# ASYLUM

by

Joshua Allen Raab

PublishAmerica
Baltimore

© 2008 by Joshua Allen Raab.
All rights reserved. No part of this book may be reproduced, stored in a retrieval system or transmitted in any form or by any means without the prior written permission of the publishers, except by a reviewer who may quote brief passages in a review to be printed in a newspaper, magazine or journal.

First printing

PublishAmerica has allowed this work to remain exactly as the author intended, verbatim, without editorial input.

All characters in this book are fictitious, and any resemblance to real persons, living or dead, is coincidental.

ISBN: 1-60563-105-1
PUBLISHED BY PUBLISHAMERICA, LLLP
www.publishamerica.com
Baltimore

Printed in the United States of America

## Dedication

*This book is dedicated to my wonderful wife Laura. Te Amo Mucho.*

# Foreword

The human heart is a place that is very much like a valley and a mountain. The valley is death and the mountain is life, both coexisting together, like day and night. When you travel from the valley up onto the mountain peak you can see that the mountain you are on is surrounded by valleys on all sides. Sometimes the mountain top becomes too cold for one to bear especially during the winter and one must descend into the valley below. This is the valley of death. To reach the next mountain peak one must always travel through the next valley. The human heart is a place much like a valley and a mountain and we are all travelers on this journey that is life.

# One

The Valley Asylum building was built in the 1920s for those who had lost their sanity during the First World War. War can create heroes but war can also create monsters. Many of the old soldiers had lost their limbs and their will to live. Many of these men had lost much more than that; they'd lost their minds. Some had committed heinous crimes against humanity; and a few had even turned to cannibalism. For almost forty years the Valley Asylum echoed with the lives and deaths of these poor, tormented souls.

In the 1960s the role of the Valley Asylum changed; it became a hospital for those much younger but just as disturbed, a children's hospital for the mentally unstable. Trapped inside the Hell that is one's own brain, these poor children carried on a lifeless existence. The simple pleasure of looking out an open window to gaze upon a sunrise or a sunset was the highlight of many a day for these young patients. The worst of the cases were strapped into their beds twenty hours a day, injected on an hourly basis with mind altering and life sucking chemicals. To say it was a bleak existence would have been one of the biggest understatements ever. Compared to the mental condition of the patients, some of the employees were even more deranged and tormented than any child trapped in that God forsaken place. It seemed that anyone could get a job at the Asylum, from Bob the Janitor who was a convicted felon and lifelong pervert, to Tammy the nurse who was addicted to Heroin and self mutilation. The head doctor and Asylum director was an unfeeling shell of a man named Thomas Henderson who, since the death of his own son, hated the sight of other children. The sound of children laughing, playing, or crying would stir a terrible rage in him, betrayed only by the throbbing of the vein in his temple. He managed to hide this dark side from most of his co-workers, despite the depth and intensity of his hatred. The smell of Juicy Fruit, or Mr. Bubble bath suds caused a churning in his stomach and a ceaseless pounding in his head that was relentless. On the inside he was tearing himself apart day by day. As the chief psychiatric doctor at

Valley Asylum for the last four years, he'd subjected himself to the constant torture that being around children had become. He often found relief in working out his anger on the children of Valley Asylum; abuse was quite common when he was on shift. He would abuse the children in the shadows when he was alone with them: a threat, a hard pinch, a slap, and sometimes worse, much worse. Dr. Henderson was a graduate of Stanford University, class of 1942, and he was also a superb golfer and an average husband. He was a walking volcano ready to explode and the villagers below never saw it coming.

Dr. Henderson was haunted by the same nightmare every time he closed his eyes. Exhaustion, alcohol, even prescription narcotics could not dull the edge of his nightly horror as he relived the death of his son over and over again. The dream never altered, never waived, it was as constant as his rage. It begins as Danny was climbing up a neighborhood Oak tree that cold winter day. A group of local teenagers decided it would be a good day to practice their aim. The boys were armed with rocks and stones; they fired them at the defenseless child, taunting him as their aim got closer and closer. Danny begged them to stop but the boys, drunk with the power that comes from feeding off of the fear of others, did not stop. They continued to throw the projectiles at the small child trapped in the tree until one stone hit Danny directly in the face causing him to fall to the ground below. He landed head first on a concrete block he'd used as a stepping stone to reach the tree's lower limbs. The air was silent as Danny and the cold ground became one. The terrified teenagers ran from the scene leaving the poor boy to bleed to death alone. Danny, however, did not die that frozen day. A woman who was walking her dog stumbled across his limp body. Had Danny been able to open his eyes, he would have seen the tear stained face of his own mother. She picked up the small, fragile body of her child and rushed him to the hospital. By some miracle, or by a cruel joke as Thomas Henderson would later come to call it, Danny's body survived but his brain did not. For two more months Danny lingered between this world and next, deep in a coma. The distraught Dr. Henderson stayed by his bedside watching his only son slowly slip into complete shadow. The ice of loss slowly formed over the good doctor's heart.

Thomas would always awake at this point from his nightmare, body wet with sweat, fear and pain almost tangible in the air around him, the sound of his own sobs in his ears with his hand outstretched to pull Danny back to him but there was no Danny to pull back.

By the time his boy finally passed away, Thomas Henderson had already begun a rapid decent down the spiraling staircase of madness. He was jealous of the living and longed for the return of his dead son. He spent many nights sitting at his son's graveside, his mind marinating in his own hatred and self-pity. He was so internally focused on his own pain and misery that he slowly crossed the line into madness without even noticing.

Dr. Henderson never found the teenagers responsible for Danny's death, and the unfulfilled desire for revenge became so strong that it began to exert itself on the innocent. God have mercy on anyone who found themselves in the path of that need, because Dr. Henderson would show none. Madness was now his only reality.

December 11, 1962

It was a cold day in December; the ground was covered with twelve inches of snow from a blizzard that had passed through the night before. It was not a pristine scene like those on the Currier and Ives tins, but a dark, gray, sludgy kind of snow that looked as if the whole world had been rendered in charcoal. The heavy air was frigid and it chilled to the bone anyone unfortunate enough to be outside in it.

Doctor Thomas Henderson ate his breakfast of champions, coffee and doughnuts, in the hospital lounge as he had done every morning for the last four years. Uncharacteristically, however, he did not finish his meal; he stood up and grabbed a large black bag that he had carried in with him. Thomas closed his blood shot eyes and wiped the sweat from his brow as he was headed for the main patient building through the long dank corridor. His shoes squeaked on the floors wet from visitors tramping in from the cold. The cold chilled one to the bone and even to the soul.

Most of the young patients had just received their daily doses of medication. He felt that the children would feel less pain if he did it now; it was an uncommonly kind thought for him. The only one he had for many years.

"Doctor Henderson what are you doing?"

A young nurse shrieked in horror as Tom pulled out a semi automatic from his bag. He began spraying bullets back and forth in the hall, killing all those who stepped into his path. A nurse stuck her head out of her patient's room and dropped to the floor with most of her face missing. Children cried, screamed, and tried to run. The sounds of innocence bleeding echoed all around him. He killed dozens of children while they were still strapped to their beds. Their miniature bodies lay there limp and lifeless. Thomas picked them off one by one until over fifty patients were slaughtered. He went from room to room, raving and incoherent, looking for more victims. Many nurses and family members died where they lay trying to protect the children including Bob the Janitor and Tammy the nurse. No soul was safe that day, no guardian Angel would intervene.

Tom came to the surgery room where a young man lay after having just received an injection of Thorazine. He locked the door behind himself and walked slowly to the limp figure on the bed; so still, so pale, so much like Danny. Dr. Henderson forced his gun into the mouth of this tiny child and the young boy suddenly awoke, dazed and frightened. The child, disturbed from his slumber and still disoriented simply stared into the red glowing eyes of the doctor. The emotional connection of the moment caused a single tear to roll down Thomas' cheek. He felt something inside him awaken, something that had died with his son, compassion.

"What am I doing?"

Thomas finally began to realize the horror of his actions. He had been a zombie for so long. The sheer magnitude of this slaughter burst through the haze that had wrapped itself around him and cleared away the remaining fog. Thomas was transfixed by the gaze of the young child.

"Not another son. Danny, please forgive me!"

Thomas finally dropped his weapon to the floor and collapsed into a fetal position. He had brought hell to earth, a very real hell. The cool floor became a comforting place for the sick man. Two armed guards punched through the door that Thomas had latched and grabbed him from off of the floor, but he was already dead. His heart, twisted and broken, could not bear up under the weight of the realization of what he'd done. The Doctor's corpse was carried away and taken to the coroner who ruled it a heart attack. An exploding heart would have been a better diagnosis. Dr. Henderson had a broken heart and a broken spirit. Finally his madness had ended.

Thomas was buried in a small plot in the back woods behind the Asylum on property the doctor had owned before his death. Only his wife attended the ceremony, the rest of his family could not bare to honor a man who was capable of such wanton cruelty. He would soon be forgotten; even his headstone was only marked with a cross. He was not buried next to his son as he had wanted, his surviving wife would not allow it.

One week after the massacre, the Asylum was closed down for good. The memories were too painful and it was thought best if the surviving patients were moved elsewhere. Death was now thick in the air and choking all those who dared to enter the Asylum. An investigation took place but no motive, other than inconsolable grief over the loss of his son, could be found. The detectives shrugged it off as a sad case of a parent driven mad by the death of his beloved son and closed the case. Dr. Henderson, however, was a far more complex man than anyone knew. If the Police department had been trying to solve the puzzle of his murders, they were missing several pieces to begin with.

Every year Thomas's wife would visit his grave on the anniversary of his death. After a few years, the doctor had become nothing more than the town's favorite scary story, an urban legend, forgotten in the onslaught of other crimes, other deaths, new tragedies and new headlines. And yet, strangely, every year eleven roses were placed on Thomas's unmarked grave, black roses. This ending was only a new beginning for the Asylum.

# Two

Dr. Smith honks his horn as two young teenagers speed by him as he enters onto Elm Street. They were the Johnson boys and they were terrible drivers. It had taken them four times to pass there drivers test. "Damn kids!"

Dr. Phil Smith had just come home from a long shift at Downtown Central Hospital. He was a pediatric doctor there. It was the end of his twentieth shift on the job. Dr. Smith lived alone in a 5000 square foot home; his only companion was Tiger his pet cat. Dr. Smith had recently gone through a messy divorce. His ex wife Cindy had taken their house in Maui and his Ferrari, poor Dr. Smith was only left with this tiny house and two BMW'S.

Phil enters his home and quickly disarms his alarm system. He was dead tired and decided that what he needed was a quick hit from his bong and a long cold shower. Phil enters his cavernous shower, big enough for the whole family, and turns on the steamy water. He reaches for his secret stash and quickly gets his bong bubbling. The night was pitch black as the phase of the new moon was above.

Tiger loved being stroked, the hands of the large bear-like man were very course and dry but Tiger liked it that way, he was never afraid of strangers. He was welcoming his new friend into his home, this, however, was not a friend at all. The shattered glass of the kitchen window covered the cold tile floor, shards extending onto the hard wood floor of the adjoining dinning room. The invader places a long shard into his pocket. The destruction of the window had gone unnoticed as Phil's shower was equipped with the latest in surround sound technology. Phil dances around the shower letting all the stresses of the day melt away inside his million dollar home.

"Roxanne, you don't have to put on..."

The intruder has quietly slipped into Dr. Smith's bedroom; he begins to rummage through the good doctor's drawers as if he were looking for something. He begins to throw socks, shirts, boxers and briefs all around the room but finds nothing else.

"Where is he hiding it?"

The man destroys the closet now looking for something. He notices a loose panel on the floor; with a swift kick he smashes the board revealing an old book and a long dagger. The large man pulls the long dagger from this secret compartment exposing this imposing instrument of death. He places the book and dagger into a duffle bag that he has brought with him. The man zips up the bag placing it on top of the doctor's dresser. He then glides silently into the bathroom where the loud sound of music can be heard and where the steamy cascade of water begins to fill his senses. He slowly grabs the shower handle and like the greatest predators in Africa he swings open the shower door ready to pounce. To his complete surprise the large shower is completely empty. The doctor has vanished without a trace, and then it happens,

"BANG."

A loud shot is heard to ring out. The bullet slices through the back of the assailant and exits quickly through his shoulder, finally lodging itself into the shower tile. The man falls to the ground, writhing in agony. Dr. Phil stands over the fallen maniac, pistol still in hand.

"You crazy bastard did you really think you could kill us all?"

Phil stands above his attacker almost taunting him. He leans closer to the fallen man, shoving the pistol in his face and stepping on his back.

"This is bigger than you Alex, you can't…"

A blood curdling noise is heard as his soft tissue is instantly destroyed with great ferocity. Phil falls over his attacker and reverts into the fetal position, steamy water covering his fallen body. The home invader drops the shard of glass from his hand and rises to his feet bleeding heavily from his back. He had narrowly escaped certain death, while the Doctor had been taunting the fallen man he had managed to slip a piece of broken glass out of his pocket and into his palm. The glass had been thrust into the man's thigh while he stood over him. Dr. Phil was dead within one minute, he had almost bled out completely. The sounds of sirens can be heard approaching in the distance and although in great pain Alex rises to his feet, he rushes to the bedroom to grab the duffle bag. In a moment he has disappeared out into the neighborhood without a trace and unseen. The police finally arrive at the scene to find the gruesome aftermath; they are only greeted by the purring of Tiger the friendly cat. The night was pitch black and the air smelled of tragedy. The evil unseen forces had already begun and the future was now uncertain for everyone.

## 1, 2003

As she awoke from her nightmare Alison screamed in terror. She was used to having these kinds of nightmares; she had experienced them her entire life. Her tiny mutt Mango, who slept by her side snuffed, rolled over, and went back to sleep. He was hardly protection from these nocturnal visions, and had taken to ignoring his mistress's unusual whimpers and shouts. Alison ran her had over her forehead, wiping the sweat from her brow. She often had this dream, at least three nights a week. In her dream, the floor would disappear sending her falling like Alice down the rabbit hole. She would hit the hard ground shooting dust clouds into the air and creating a giant smoke screen around her body.

When she looked around this strange place she could see men wearing dark black cloaks. These monsters would reveal their faces to her, showing hideous deformities. The flesh of these creatures would be hanging loosely on their bodies and would occasionally fall completely off of their decrepit skeletons. They just stood there looking at Alison as if she were a Thanksgiving turkey. Then in a frenzied rush, the cloaked figures would attack her all at once and begin to rip her apart. She would wake up screaming and kicking, much to Mango's consternation as he often landed on the floor after her flailing. These dreams were the types of things that made her take up coffee drinking as her full-time job, leaving journalism as her second career. She felt cursed by these visions, but had suffered under them so long she no longer bothered to contemplate their meaning.

"Loose wiring," she muttered for the hundredth time and laid back into her pillow. Sometimes she wished she didn't need to sleep, ever.

Alison was a reporter for the Valley Chronicle. Her specialty was digging up the worst in human nature, which as she found out, was very easy to do because everyone had a dark side to reveal. She could expose it, get the bad guys in trouble, and get rich in the process. Alison also wrote mystery novels based on cases she would investigate. She never seemed to have enough time to write enough to make her publisher happy, as investigative journalism was her true love, but she tried to pound out a few chapters of her current novel whenever she had the chance.

She loved being single and having her freedom. She loved the fact that if she wanted to walk around her apartment naked and drink milk straight from the carton she could do it—and at the same time, too. There would be no nagging boyfriend to control her and no bratty kids needing a diaper change. She was free to leave at a moment's notice to follow whatever leads she might find in her latest investigation. It was her curious nature that often got her into trouble, but this nature also got her onto the front page, and subsequently into this great apartment and behind the wheel of the classic sports car in the garage downstairs. Alison was by far the best reporter in the state; at least that's what she kept telling herself.

"Oh shit, I'm supposed to meet mom for lunch at one o'clock." Alison jumped into her shower, quickly dressed her agile frame in jeans and a slightly wrinkled button down shirt, and threw an Indians ball cap over her long brunette pony tail so that the entire world wouldn't have to suffer through a bad hair day with her. She grabbed her keys, ran out the door and almost tripped over her own feet as she made a mad dash for her car. She hopped into her 1965 Cherry Red Mustang, punched the automatic garage door opener, gunned the engine and left a trail of rubber behind her as she rocketed out into the waiting street. Without a backwards glance, she hit the button on the remote clipped to her visor and was around the corner before the garage door had fully closed.

"I hope she's still there, I'm almost a half hour late." She floored the pony hoping the local yokel police force was not around the next corner setting up a major sting operation to meet their quota of traffic stops for the month. She figured that if she were pulled over the cop would recognize her, maybe ask for an autograph, and then send her on her way with a warning.

Picking up her phone she hit the memory key and drummed her fingers impatiently on the steering wheel as she waited. The phone rang twice and was answered by a voice that could only be described as "aging surfer dude".

"What's up, this is John."

"Hey John, it's Alison. Got a hot story for me?"

"Hey Ally baby, que paso? I got just what you're looking for. It's a real gem!"

A huge smile spread across Alison's face. "That's just what I wanted to hear. Spill the beans Johnny!"

John paused dramatically and then replied, "I want you to interview this guy named Alex Hoard. You've heard of him right?"

A mental image of a large man covered in tattoos and carrying a chainsaw came to mind as she eased the Mustang through a tight turn.

"You mean Alex Hoard the doctor killer? Big guy, tattoos, chainsaw…killed over thirty doctors in less then a month?"

John laughed, "The one and only. I think this could be huge for you if you cover it right. He is scheduled to be executed soon and we have an exclusive, how we got this chance, I don't know, but I'm giving it to you! When can you come in for the info?"

Alison checked her watched, "I'll come by the office later; I gotta go meet Mama O'Connell for lunch."

"Ok, see you later. Ciao, Ally."

Alison hung up the phone just in time to see the red and blue flashing lights of a police cruiser in her rearview mirror. She looked at her speedometer,

"Holy shit, eighty miles an hour." Slamming on the brakes, she pulled the Mustang onto the shoulder. The officer slowly got out of the cruiser and headed over to a very nervous Alison.

"Maybe if I show this cop a little cleavage he'll go easy on me," Alison prayed as she surreptitiously tried to get the top buttons of her shirt undone while pushing her breasts up in her bra to get a better effect. The officer knocked on the closed window causing Alison to jump and sending her bosom right back to where it came from. Alison lowered the window to reveal a female police officer standing there. Alison's sexy smile turned into a giant frown as she gazed up into the face of the Amazonian woman before her. "I thought this kind of crap only happened in bad movies", she thought as she tried to look innocent and greeted the officer.

"You know how fast you were going, Ma'am?"

Alison smiled, "About 70?"

The officer stared at Alison intently and then blurted out, "Hey you're Alison O'Connell. 'The' Alison O'Connell! I love your articles. I've read them all. I think I have to qualify as your biggest fan in the world." Alison began to feel a little relief as her 'big fan theory' seemed to be playing itself out.

"Thanks! I'm so glad you appreciate my work, Officer....Ridjeck." Alison oozed charm as she read the officer's badge and smiled.

"Remember the article you wrote about cheating husbands and how to catch them?" the eager Officer Ridjeck asked. Alison nodded. "Well I used your trap and caught my own husband cheating. Needless to say, he is history now."

Alison now covered in a complete fake smile muttered, "Good for you!" What she really thought was "Someone actually married this Zena wannabe? This woman makes Ernest Borgnine look like Ms. America."

Catching a glimpse of her watch, Alison was reminded of how late she was and began to explain why she was speeding.

The officer laughed, "I totally understand, I'm very close with my mother. Moms are very important people to have around." She lifted up her little clipboard, "Let me just give you this ticket so you can be on your way then."

The chin of Ms. Alison O'Connell, usually raised in a defiant and cocky tilt, dropped to the floor with a resounding thud. "She is actually going to give me a ticket! What a complete bitch," Alison fumed as she snapped her mouth shut and ground her teeth together.

The officer reached into her pocket for a small piece of paper. "Hey Ms. O'Connell, could I get your autograph so I can put it on my mantle?"

Amazed at the woman's gall, Alison signed the ticket and then smiled sweetly at the officer, "There ya go; now you have my autograph right here on the ticket, so photo-copy it if ya need any more." Officer friendly grabbed the ticket from Alison and returned to her squad car without another word. Alison threw her copy of the ticket into the backseat with a mumbled "Most expensive autograph I've ever given. Talk about an ego check." In no time, she had the Mustang back up to eighty.

Twenty minutes later she finally reached Bambinos, her mother's favorite Mexican restaurant known for their enchiladas and their loaded margaritas. Spotting her mom on the patio, Alison snuck up and wrapped her arms around her. Mrs. O'Connell was a frail woman standing a meager 5'0" and weighing between ninety-five and one hundred pounds at any given time. Her brunette hair was liberally sprinkled with white and her warm brown eyes danced with happiness at the arrival of her only daughter.

"Hey mommy, sorry I'm so late; Cops and robbers and all that good stuff." Said Alison apologetically as she squeezed her mom and inhaled her perfume. Windsong, a classic…just like mom, she thought.

Patting her daughter's arm lovingly, Mama O'Connell excused her daughter's tardiness with the patient acceptance of one who'd done it a thousand times before. "It's alright dear. I'm just glad you made it."

Alison pulled a picture from her purse and slid it across the bright red vinyl tablecloth to her mother. "Here, this is for you it's an old family picture I found. It shows you, dad and Jeremy. I guess I wasn't born yet."

Mrs. O'Connell's eyes flicked to Alison's and then she lifted the photograph off the table, their fingers brushing in the exchange. She stared through the picture clearly remembering the exact moment the picture was originally taken.

"Where did you find this?"

"Sorry mom I can't reveal my sources," Alison said around a mouthful of chips and salsa and was surprised to see a few tears roll quietly down her mother's face.

"Your brother looked just like you, Alison. You were practically identical twins." The older woman sighed, "I miss them Alison. I miss them everyday. It's just us girls now."

Alison reached over the table to clasp her mother's hand in hers worried by the frail feel of it in her own stronger, calloused hand. "It's ok, mommy, it's not your fault. We still have each other."

Mrs. O'Connell gave Alison a watery smile and let go of her hand as a waiter appeared with the food she'd ordered while waiting for Alison. "Thank you Ali. I just wish that your brother…he was so young, too young to pass…such an awful fever."

"I know its hard, mom, but I am here for you. I know that I never really knew my brother but I feel his loss too. I always wanted to have a big brother to take care of me and look after me, especially that time that those girls put gum in my hair in the third grade."

As Alison had hoped, the mention of a favorite family memory drew a smile from her mother. "Your father was so proud of you; I wish he would have made it to see you become such a big reporter. His heart just couldn't take it."

Alison lowered her eyes and said softly, "The funeral last year was one of the hardest things I ever had to go through. It was so sad to sit there knowing he was gone." "I know sweetheart me too." Mom smiled at the top of Ali's head. "Your father loved us so much and he was always so understanding." She looked again at the images in the picture and kissed them, "Always understanding."

The two women were quiet for a while, eating their lunches and allowing the painful topic to settle. Before long they were chatting like girlfriends, mostly about nothing. They were good at having long conversations about absolutely nothing. Eventually, after more chips, a couple of margaritas, and some tasty caramel-topped cheesecake, the pleasant afternoon came to an end.

Walking her mother to her car, Alison heard a sniffle and turned to see her mother weeping gently. "Mom why are you crying?"

"I'm ok dear; it's just the pain of old memories coming back." She looked Alison directly in her eyes. "Have I been a good mother Ally?"

Confused but wanting to erase the insecure and frightened sound in her mother's voice, Alison grabbed her mother and they embraced, "You are the best. I am the luckiest girl on the planet."

Mrs. O'Connell wiped the tears from her face, "I just wish that I had the strength to tell you more about our past. Oh listen to me being a big silly. Don't mind this old lady…I'm fine."

Alison squeezed her mother tightly, "I just want you to be happy; I don't want the past to haunt you forever. I love you."

Smiling, Mama O'Connell pulled away and gently brushed Alison's hair back from her forehead, "Thank you Alison that means so much to me, be careful dear."

Alison walked back to her car, saddened by her mother's display of sentiment. By the time she'd buckled her seatbelt, she'd set aside her concerns about her mother and turned her thoughts to her upcoming interview. After all, it's not every day you got to interview a mass murderer.

# Three

Raider maximum-security prison, she could see it now in the distance. It was an old army stockade that looked as if it should have been condemned at least twenty years ago. The prison was forlorn and dark; not the place for a summer holiday, at least that's what the butterflies in her stomach said. She felt a large lump in her throat and realized that she was scared to death. The realization troubled her, as she was not the "girly" type, and scared wasn't in her vocabulary.

"Now if I could just convince my stomach of that," she thought, irritated at her shaky nerves. "I have to keep it together; this story could make me big." Getting into the spirit of her own pep talk, Alison grinned, "Barbara Walters is gonna be my bitch when I get done with this story. Look out America, say hello to the next Pulitzer Prize winner. This could be huge." The butterflies settled down, and she pushed the Mustang back to a roar.

High above, the heavy black clouds were rolling and a deep rumble could be felt as well as heard. The smell of rain hung in the air and the impending storm pressed down upon the prison. Glancing nervously at the darkened sky, Alison turned on the radio looking for a distraction. The smooth melodies of CCR filled the Mustang.

"I see a bad moon rising, I see trouble on the way," she quickly flipped stations finding an all eighties station. "I always feel like somebody's watching me." Alison turned off the radio and began to sing to herself, "Doe a deer a female deer." Out of the corner of her eye Alison spotted two children playing catch by the side of the road.

"Maybe there's a trailer park out here or something," She thought to herself, cursing the stupidity of parents who would let their children play so close to the road.

With a shake of her head, Alison focused again on her upcoming interview. "Hello Mr. Hoard. No,no,no." Alison cleared her throat. "Good evening Alex.

UGH! I sound like a game show host. Fuck it, I'll just wing it." Rain fell in fat heavy drops, obscuring the view of the road ahead as Alison fumbled to get the windshield wipers turned on. A bolt of lightning slammed into the mountain with a resounding roar of thunder setting Alison's heart racing.

Twenty minutes and several show tunes and commercial jingles later, Alison pulled into the prison, nerves wound tightly thanks to the storm and a deep sense of foreboding. A large, burly guard carrying a nightstick greeted Alison from the shack positioned between the two large gates that lead up the hill to the prison's main buildings. As she approached, he motioned for her to roll her window down. She squinted up through the rain at him as he spoke.

"Howdy Ms. O'Connell, we've been expecting you. Beautiful weather we're having." As quick as he had finished his sentence a tall under fed man wearing too much cologne popped up on the other side of the car,

"Wow it's really you!" Alison almost jumped out of her skin, startled by the emaciated guard in a yellow rain slicker.

Irritated more at herself than at the guards, her response was a gruff, "Ok, that was not funny. Just tell me where I need to park." Seeing the crestfallen look on the second guards' face, and not wanting to alienate a potential source, Alison pasted on her best smile and added a "Please."

The large guard's smile popped back into place and he pointed to the other guard, "That is Skinny Boy Ed he'll show you where to park. Follow him around through the special entrance." Ed hopped into a covered golf cart and began to drive toward a sub-terrain tunnel. Alison followed him into the black mouth of the stone archway; only the flickering of weak yellow wall lights illuminated their way. The air inside the tunnel smells as if someone had dumped their refuse all over the ground. She could distinctly detect the odor of burnt rubber mixed with what she thought was human fecal matter. Alison covers her nose in disgust,

"They're leading me into the center of the earth or at least New Jersey!" Glancing at the trance inducing tunnel wall Alison sees what appears to be the face of a child. The chalky features are very distinguishable against the black brick lining the tunnel. She swerves her car almost nailing the side of the tunnel wall.

"Holy shit, what was that?" The face of another child appears in Alison's rearview window but disappears right before she can turn her eyes to notice the visage. The brakes of the Mustang screech as she applies her entire one hundred and twenty-pound frame onto them. Alison raises her head and is startled to see that she has reached the end of the tunnel. Ed jumps from his golf cart,

"We're here Ms. O'Connell. He smiles at Alison, "At least we know your brakes work!" The skinny man begins to roll over with laughter. Alison raises her middle finger letting skinny Ed know that she thinks he is number one! Alison looks back down the tunnel to where she saw the thing.

"I'm sure whatever I saw was just a trick of light and shadow against the tunnel wall, besides ghosts don't exist anyway!" She takes a deep breath and turns off her car. Alison and Ed walk over to the bob-wire gated entrance and with a buzzing noise the massive structure swings open.

"This is where we keep all the really dangerous ones." Was this supposed to make her feel safer she wondered? It was the wrong thing to say at the wrong time.

Alison steps into the main hall of the subterranean prison compound. The room was like something she had seen in an old horror flick when she was a little girl. There was one problem; this was no movie! The long hallway ended at a single cell. Ed points to the room and slowly shakes his head.

"That's where it sleeps." Alison takes a big gulp and begins to walk toward the room. The smell she had experienced earlier in the tunnel was now magnified ten times. The two reach Alex's door, Ed pushes Alison aside and stands in front of her.

"Hold on Ma'am I need to sedate and shackle it." Alison looks at Ed with disgust.

"IT, is he not a human anymore?"

Ed replies, "Ma'am he's not even an animal. It's a monster!" In a flash of terror an arm shots through the small food tray hole located in the center of the cell door. The sharp fingernails looking like those of a cougar, the thick hair on the arm like that of a black bear. The hand grabs Ed's neck in an icy grip squeezing the life out of him. In an almost unintelligible language Ed begins to scream at Alison.

"Grab the needle!" He points at a black bag on the floor. "Hurry!" Alison, now terrified, clumsily opens the case and takes out a long needle.

She yells at Ed, "Now what?" Alison's adrenaline is now racing out of control. He points to the man's arm and makes a jabbing motion.

"Stick him!" She plunges the needle into his arm, pushing the fluid deep into his blood stream. Alison drops the needle onto the moldy floor and covers her mouth. Alex slowly releases Ed and a large thump is heard behind the prisoner's cell door as he comes crashing to the Earth. A second guard finally arrives and the two men enter the cell of Alex Hoard and shackle him to a steel chair. Ed turns to Alison, rubbing his sore neck.

"He's all yours Lady. We'll be right outside the door. He's harmless now that we've tied him down. Trust me he ain't going nowhere." The guard turns his attention to Alex. "He'll be awake in a second." Ed punches Alex's face for good measure, knocking a tooth loose. Alison gathers her composure after being scared to death.

A few moments later the prisoner lifts his head exposing his scarred face complete with a missing eye. The Cyclops looks directly at Alison who was standing a good distance from him. At first he just moans and then finally speaks.

"Who are you lady?" Alison begins to stutter.

"I'm, I'm, I'm Alison O'Connell from the Valley Chronicle. I'm here to ask you a few questions and if there is anything that you want to share then please feel free." He looks her in the eye and begins to grin sarcastically.

"How about my pain?" Alex lunges at Alison but is prevented by the chains from reaching her. She gulps for air and leaps back about six more feet. She straightens her skirt then turns on her mini recorder and with her heart in her throat she begins to speak.

"I, I have a few questions to ask you Mr. Hoard so I'll just begin. Ok? Why did you do it? Why kill all those Doctors?" Alex smiles and spits to the floor; his spit burning a hole in the wood like acid. The prisoner grins again.

"I was the hand of God punishing the wicked men of the eclipse. Those men will never hurt anyone else again. The mirror has been reversed." For the first time during the so-called interview Alex relaxes in his chair, "You are familiar to me. You remind me of my mother, the mother who never came looking for me." Alison notices her recorder has stopped recording, she shakes it back and forth realizing that the machine has begun to eat her tape slowly. This has not been her day, what else could go wrong?

"Why is my recorder going crazy?" She turns her focus back to Alex Hoard as he begins to shake in convulsions; streams of a strange blue fluid begin to roll down his glazed face originating from some unseen source on his forehead.

"Please don't hurt me!" Alex's voice has now changed into that of a frightened child. Alison becomes amazed in this instant transformation and it is hard for her to believe her own ears. His voice is completely different; it is as if he is possessed. Alison shakes her recorder again hoping that it will start recording. She begins to inch closer to the inmate but still staying her distance. She felt like a snake handler now.

"What happened to you Alex?" The man begins to cry like a child, "I am not Alex Hoard I am y…." The voice stops suddenly. A trance like look now covers his face. The inner turmoil seems to be tearing this sad soul apart. Alison quickly writes down what the prisoner is saying in her backup notebook, pressing very hard on her notepad. Thank God she brought it she thought to herself. Alex begins to shake again, this time with more jolting force. A mini earthquake rattles through her bones as Alex continues to shake.

"Someone help me, Daddy is…." The strange blue substance begins dripping from the man's mouth. "What the hell is that!" Alison is horrified but she can't seem to look away. This is all so bizarre to her. She surveys Alex's entire body and is drawn to a tattoo on the man's arm so she decides to try to sketch it on her notepad. The large tattoo reads B.E. A picture of a lighting bolt runs between the two large letters. Alison's heartbeat has now doubled in pace. The emotions inside her small frame begin to drown out any sense of sanity she may have had before this strange encounter began. All control has been lost. Houston we have a major problem!

Alex begins to shout random words at the top of his lungs, "Father, trapped, sacrifice, my brothers, blood baptism." The two guards who were standing outside the room charge through the door after hearing the screaming of the prisoner Alex Hoard.

"Ma'am are you ok?" Alison turns her head to speak to them.

"He's leaking something blue and he just started yelling. I think he is having a seizure." She turns back to focus her attention on the prisoner but he somehow has moved much closer to her. Alex Hoard is now standing two inches from her; he has managed to escape his shackles and the chair that had held him so securely only moments ago. At the sight of this man so close to her Alison quickly falls to the ground. Alex begins to speak to her now in a banshee like high-pitched voice, his body surrounded with a bright blue glow. An unseen force blew his hair around his head like a strong wind.

"Through them he is returning soon. Flesh of my flesh. It must be stopped." In an instant his body burst into flames before her very eyes, charred pieces of his flesh flew through the air landing all around the room, it was like witnessing a suicide bomber up close. Alison had to cover her face to avoid being burned. She screams for help as loud as her voice would allow, still covering her face with a tight grip. A guard shakes her arm frantically.

"Ma'am, Ma'am are you alright?" She screams again like a banshee then out of instinct opens her eyes to see that she is inside the prison tunnel near the underground entrance. She is no longer inside the actual room of the burning man. Was it a dream?

"Ma'am are you ready to go see the prisoner now?"

"WHAT?" What was he talking about; she had already seen him, hadn't she? Alison looks at the guard. "I feel very sick all of a sudden. I don't think I can do this interview." She jumps back into her car and turns it around, peeling out inside the tunnel, heading toward the prison exit. "I've lost it!" It all seemed so real, she could vividly remember it all. As she nears the exit gate of the prison she happens to look down to her passenger seat for a brief second where her notepad catches her eye. On the pad the words "B.E." and "through them he will." are scribbled, the worst part was that it was not written in her handwriting, it was someone else's handwriting. Alison could feel her lunch now entering her throat. It would soon be time for another car wash, especially for the interior. She speeds past the front guard shack where two guards stood shaking their heads as the daredevil races by

"I never could understand those reporter types. She was supposed to interview that Psycho Alex Hoard but she acted like she just saw a ghost or something." Alison drove like a bat out of hell all the way home. She needed to be somewhere she felt safe, somewhere she felt secure, Alison needed to go home. She didn't understand what was going on but instinctively she wanted to find out. Things were beginning to get very strange very quick. Alison was always looking for a big story, but it looked like the big story was also looking for her this time.

# Four

"It's bigger then I had imagined," thought Tyler Hoffman as he pulled up to the gate of the old building. It was much older looking compared to his former mental image.

"We're here sir," the driver shouts into the back of the stretch limo. The tall thin man opens his door and steps out onto the overgrown dusty road. Tyler Hoffman is the biggest real-estate mogul in the country; and a pretty good businessman too.

"Well, with a little work this old complex will become the next multi-million dollar babysitter for the World's most messed up rich kids. We'll help make them into respectful boys and girls. The future leaders of America." The driver steps over to close the door behind Tyler.

"Excuse me for asking sir, but what do you mean by a babysitter for the rich?" Tyler laughs, lights a cigar, then replies.

"Well my portly servant, I am going to turn this into a summer retreat where only the richest aristocrats will send their spoiled brat children. Who else would you trust with your children if not me?" He raises his hands to create a frame around the building. "I can just picture it, swimming pools in the back. Horseback riding over there, Volleyball courts on the other side, and oh yes my private offices up there in that splendid tower. I just love children. They are nature's little sponge"

The driver now scratching his head replies, "Excuse me again sir, but didn't this building use to be a mental Asylum many years ago?"

Tyler looks sternly at the chubby driver, "A long, long time ago! The past is dead and gone, I'm here and I'm alive! Besides I got the property at basement prices." The face of Tyler Hoffman has now become completely red with anger. The driver let's out a fake chuckle then returns to staring at his dirty shoes. Tyler walks over to the towering main front gate and looks up. The fence stands at over ten feet tall dwarfing the six foot four Tyler Hoffman. Each side of the fence weighs over four hundred pounds easily. Atop each half of the fence sits a web covered stone gargoyle. The creatures sit looming over all that choose to pass through these massive gate structures.

"When I get done with these kids, they're gonna make Richie Cunningham look like Charles Manson. Senators, Athletes, Hollywood moguls, and shady business men are all gonna pay top dollar to let their kids play with Uncle Tyler." A huge grin now covers his face stretching from ear to ear, as if he were hiding a diamond that was about to burst forth from his mouth.

"This spot will do just fine; opening these gates for business will only open other gates for me in the future!" The driver looks toward Tyler now completely confused, why would Tyler choose this location when there was plenty of prime real estate elsewhere. He was paid to drive and not to think.

Beyond the gate a large courtyard extended a few hundred yards back into the main Asylum building. Old and dried up water fountains and cracked stone statues of gothic lore filled the courtyard and added a very ancient feel to the property. The Asylum compound consists of three major buildings: the main hospital building in the center surrounded by two additional administrative buildings on each side. A giant tower extends heavenward from the main hospital building while a large plush forest surrounds the entire premise. The forest has covered this tragic place for more then forty years now, growing deeper into the heart of the Asylum compound. A long narrow stream extends halfway around the backside of the Asylum, the water has taken on a very dark shade of blue, and some would say almost a black hue. The old Valley graveyard containing the remains of fourteen people sits less then two hundred yards from the backside of the main hospital building. The remains date between 1865 and 1962. A low blanket of fog consistently covers the cemetery floor creating dancing forms in the sunlight and the moonlight. This site was going to take an extreme makeover to turn it into a happy fun place for kids. Tyler seemed undaunted by the task that lay before him. He would bring this cold place back to life if it was the last thing he did. The very last thing he did.

Tyler takes a huge puff of his stogie; "In less then two weeks this place is gonna look like Club Med." A cool breeze blows from out of the nearby oak forest sending chills up his spine. In a flash the sky seems to turn from blue to blood red, clouds begin to roll in. This impromptu storm seems to be centered over the old Asylum itself. Tyler watches the moving clouds intently. In a vicious strike a bolt of lightning crashes down hitting the giant Asylum tower sending pieces of stone crashing down. Tyler falls on his ass; startled by the celestial event, he then quickly jumps to his feet.

"It's time to go!" The two men hurry into the limo and make a hasty retreat back to the highway reaching 100 mph in seconds.

Tyler reaches into an overhead compartment and pulls out a gold plated cell phone. Everything he owned was gold plated much like his ego. Tyler hits his office button on the phone and places it to his ear. Static can be heard, and then a growling voice fills his ear.

"The spirits are coming for you!" Tyler at hearing this voice drops the phone to the floor.

"Holy shit, I knew I shouldn't have taken all those uppers this morning. I'm hearing voices now." Tyler picks up the discarded phone, this time a woman's voice answers.

"I got you good that time didn't I Mr. Hoffman? I knew you were going to check out that new project. It used to be an old Asylum and all. I thought you'd get a kick out of a little ghost humor." Janet laughs ferociously.

Tyler replies in kind, laughing like a weasel, "A new secretary with a sense of humor, I like that. Do it again and your ass will be out in the street looking for a new job!" Tyler clears his throat and continues to speak, "I need you to cancel all my afternoon meetings and get the boys out to my newest project ASAP. I've got deadlines to meet here. I have people who expect me to finish this project. Did anyone important call for me today?"

Janet now cautiously replies, "Yes sir your wife called."

He switches the phone from his right ear to his left, "Tell her I'm still in Japan on business. I don't want her to know that I am still in town. Am I crystal?"

Janet replies, "Yes sir, oh and Jennifer called too."

Tyler takes another large puff on his Cuban cigar, "Good, good, tell her I'll see her tonight! Oh and Janet if you ever pull a stunt like that again, I'll murder you slowly, bury your body where no one can find it and piss on your grave. Have a nice day!" Tyler hangs up his phone and lights a second cigar. He takes a double drag, "Soon I'll be having visions of sugar-plums dancing in my head." The sky above still shows tints of red stretching across the horizon like veins across a broken body.

The tossing and turning of young Alison in her bed sends her little puppy Mango crashing to the floor below. He hits the ground and scampers off into the kitchen. Mango releases a loud bark waking Alison instantly.

"What, what?" Alison looks around her room. "Mango is that you?" She crawls out of bed and walks into her bathroom. Alison stands in front of her mirror and stares at her reflection, "What's wrong with me? I'm the only woman over thirty who still needs a nightlight. I think I am going nuts." She turns on the faucet and begins to splash cool water onto her face. The reflection of a black-cloaked figure appears behind Alison in the mirror. She is too busy splashing the liquid into her eyes to even notice. A long pale boney hand extends from the dark figure inching slowly toward Alison's throat, the fingernails elongating as they near her. She lifts her head again to peer into the mirror, but the figure has vanished into the darkness. Alison grabs a towel and dries her face.

"I need to get some sleep tonight, enough with these nightmares already. I gotta have a Valium around here somewhere." Alison walks back into her room. She notices her window is slightly open, she found it a bit odd because it had been closed earlier. A strong breeze enters the bedroom and begins blowing the long white curtains around like two dancing lovers in the moonlight.

Alison walks over to close it; she reaches over to grab the latch, "RING, RING." The unexpected sound of the phone ringing nearly scares Alison out of her open window and onto the wet concrete below. She closes the window tightly then picks up the phone.

"Hello, hello, hi mom, you just startled me that's all. Is everything ok, why are you calling so late?" Without warning a surge of blue light shoots through the room, like a comet crashing into the earth. The blinding light vanishes in a second. Alison picks up the phone that she had dropped on the floor when the illumination event occurred.

"Mom something weird just happened. Mom are you still there?" The voice on the phone is still there, only it is now a deep throaty voice and no longer the voice of her mother.

"The blood is the key." Alison screams in terror. The walls of her room, like Jell-O, begin to undulate all around her. The floor under her feet becomes sticky like molasses and the air fills with the stench of burning flesh. Alison is pulled onto the floor by her overwhelming fear. Her body now completely covered in some mysterious sticky substance. The sheets of her bed begin to move as if small bodies lay squirming underneath them. She let's out a piercing cry for help, but there is no response.

Suddenly her covers fly up to the ceiling and four children covered in blood spring to the floor mere inches from the paralyzed reporter, surrounding her completely. Their eyes black and hollow, their skin pale white and covered in thick red blood. The blood oozes from every orifice leaving red pools all over her bedroom floor. With all her strength Alison grits and pulls herself to her feet the unknown ooze burning holes into her calves as she completes this miracle of standing up again, the horrified woman runs to the door and grabs the handle, she swings it open. As the hinges swing open an all engulfing flood of blood splashes down sending her flying back to the sticky ground.

"BZZZZZZZ, BZZZZZZZZZ." Alison screams again; this time waking her from a deep sleep. She realizes that this had been another nightmare, but this one seemed a little too real even for her, the sheets of the bed drenched with sweat. She grips her blanket and curls into the fetal position a new wave of tears begin to stream from her eyes. Alison peers out of her bedroom window, her only comfort was the fact that the sun was shinning brightly in the sky and she had made it through the night.

Two hours after this extreme nightmare Alison arrives late to work, visibly shaken and looking like shit. She notices a stretch limousine parked outside the front entrance so she drives around it spotting a custom license plate, it reads, "BIG T." She new it was the pretty boy millionaire and all around scum bag Tyler Hoffman. He often graced the Valley Chronicle's presence, after all, he was banging the owner's daughter, oh and she was only nineteen. Alison parks her Stang, grabs her trusty notebook and heads to her office. She has a ton of research to do on the life of Alex Hoard in a short amount of time. As Alison enters the revolving doors of the Chronicle building a few drops of blood fall from her notebook but this goes completely unnoticed. The rabbit hole began to go much deeper now but Alison was finding more than rabbits waiting at the other end of the tunnel.

# Five

As Alison walked into her office, her home away from home; from across the hall she heard a very familiar voice.

"Hey Ally baby, how are ya babe?" It was John Bobecker, her forty-year-old boss. He still thought he was eighteen and on a good day he acted about nineteen and a half. He was forever the missing beach boy mixed with a little Peter Fonda. Sandals, Bermuda shorts and a Hawaiian shirt was his normal attire.

Alison smiles, "Hey John-boy, I see Big T is here today."

"Oh yeah he just bought the old Valley Asylum building and as we speak they are turning it into a country club for dysfunctional rich kids."

Alison laughs, "Hmm, I wonder why he's blessing us with his presence today? I mean besides screwing everything with two legs!" John smiles back and gives her the universal sign for when two people are screwing each other's brains out, Index finger through the ol' hole.

She laughs like a hyena and then replies; "He's visiting Jennifer huh?" Jennifer Peterson is the daughter and heir to the Valley Chronicle; her father William Peterson is the current owner of the newspaper and a very wealthy man.

"That's right visiting!" A booming voice from behind Alison states in a very assertive tone. She turns to see Tyler J. Hoffman standing there. The big grease ball himself sporting his custom European suit, gold rim glasses and derby hat. He grabs Alison's hand, "Hello Alison, you look like you haven't slept in days, it reminds me of when we used to date." He reaches down and kisses her hand, "Maybe one day you'll finally decide to put me in one of your scary novels. I could be the brave hero or something." She pulls her hand back.

"Or something! Excuse me gentlemen, and I use that word loosely, I have work to do." Alison enters her office slamming the door in Tyler's face.

"She wants me." Tyler scoffs, "She wants me."

John shakes his head, "Yeah sure she does about as much as you want your wife."

Tyler steps right in front of John's face, "You haven't changed much since college have you?" Tyler pats John on the head, "You are still the same closed-minded ignorant slob!"

John replies," You haven't changed either Tyler! You are still an asshole!" The two exchange an aggressive silent stare. The long legs of a beautiful girl now enter Tyler's field of vision, he clears his throat and walks toward the woman.

Tyler turns his head towards John, "You're lucky my friend is here, we have some briefs to go over now, stay safe Johnny!" Tyler kisses the girl on the cheek and the two walk into the elevator.

John wipes the drool from his chin after seeing the silicon beauty, "He must have sold his soul to have his kind of lifestyle but that would imply that he had a soul to begin with."

Alison sits at her desk and thinks to herself, "Why would Alex target only Doctors?" She turns on her computer and goes to her police report search engine. With a few strokes the life story of Mr. Hoard appears right before her eyes. She begins to read over it slowly sipping her coffee intently, "Let's see here, born March 11, 1955. He was the younger of two brothers, born in Houston Texas. He was diagnosed with several mental disorders by age seven. He checked into, holy crap!" Alison pulls her chair nearer to the screen making her close enough to lick the screen if she had wanted to, "It says he checked into Valley Asylum May 21, 1962." She sits back into her chair, "Wow that's forty years ago, almost to the day." She takes a big breath, "This is too weird!" Alison was now in deep thought.

"Everything Alright Ally?" Alison in an instinctive reaction throws her arms back spilling her coffee all over Johns' crotch. He screams in agony! The beach boy had caught her off guard and snuck up from behind.

"If anyone else sneaks up from behind me this week I'm gonna strangle them!"

John rubs his head, "Take it easy babe. You almost burnt my balls off. Ya know they make pills to relax individuals such as yourself who are going through stress or not getting enough sex!" He smiles with a shit-eating grin drying his groin with a hand towel.

Alison turns back to her computer screen, "Sorry John, I've just had a crazy couple of days. What do you know about the Valley Asylum? I've heard stories as a child but I don't remember much."

John scratches his ever-expanding forehead, "hmm, I think it closed down in the early sixties when some Doctor went crazy and killed a bunch of patients."

Alison stands up from her chair, "Are you serious John? I thought that story was just an old wives' tale. Alex Hoard was a patient there around the same time. I'm not sure when he left but I need to find out more about him and this doctor who went mad." She gets up from her chair and walks over to the door, "click"; she locks the bolt then turns to face John. "Ok, John I have to tell you something."

John lifts his eyebrows and replies, "This should be interesting Ally. You're not an alien, are ya?" She returns to her chair and slowly sits down trying not to burn herself with the puddle of spilled coffee.

"John, I've been seeing things lately, ghosts, visions, I don't know what they are, but it's scaring me." A look of fear falls over John's leathery face.

"You're joking right? I mean you're pulling my leg!"

She shakes her head, "No John, I haven't even told my mother yet either. When I went to visit Alex Hoard something weird happened. It was like I was there but I wasn't. He burst into flames right before my eyes John! I can't explain it; just know that it would scare the white off of Vanilla Ice." John's face is now completely pale.

"You're not gonna do what I think you're gonna do? Are ya?" A huge knot has now formed in his throat.

"John, I need to get into the Valley Asylum building. I just wanna check out the premises for clues or something. I just feel like there is something for me to find there."

He puts his hands up to his face; "No way, I'm not going near there, especially if you are already seeing things. No way Sherlock!" John begins pacing, "At least at Wood Stock we didn't mind seeing weird things. LSD trips were as close as I got to seeing ghosts." John paces back and forth like a wind up toy.

A huge smile develops over Alison's face, "Great, it's settled then, I'll meet you here at midnight tonight! Oh and John, bring a flashlight." She kisses him on the forehead then leaves the room. The fat man now standing completely still like a stop sign.

John puts his hands over his eyes, "Oh God, why me? I was going to wax my surfboard tonight. Maybe make some brownies!"

# Six

May 22, 2001

"I can't believe I'm doing this," John thought to himself as he watched Alison finally pull up to the front of the Chronicle building. Alison turns off her engine and hops out of her car.

"What took ya so long babe? It's almost 12:30." Alison is now unloading her trunk of its many contents.

"Sorry John but a girl's gotta be prepared for her first felony ya know?"

John walks over to his black van, "Let's get this over with babe." He has the expression on his face of a young girl getting ready to have her kidney removed. Alison hops into the passenger seat and the two take off for their midnight rendezvous with the Valley Asylum.

"Nice van John, I'd think with your salary you'd be driving a Ferrari, not to mention you'd have a thicker hairline." She laughs under her breath.

John's face sours, "Hey, Hey, come on Ally, keep 'em above the belt, would ya? This is an exact replica of the van used in the TV show 'A-Team.' It's a classic!"

Alison bursts out into sudden laughter; "I pity the poor fool!" This time they both fill their bellies with laughter, but the happy feelings don't last long.

"Holy shit!" The van swerves off the road almost hitting a telephone pole, but John manages to return the van to the street a mere two inches before a brush with disaster.

"What are you doing John?" Alison looks in the rearview to see a deserted road behind them.

"Sorry Ally, I swear I saw a little girl standing in the road. Didn't you see her? She was bouncing a ball or something." John shakes his head, "Great, now we're both seeing things!" John begins to recite some prayers quietly then make the sign of the cross. "Twenty years of Catholic school and I thought those nuns were scary. That little girl looked like she was wearing a straight jacket and covered in bullet holes." Up in the distance the outline of the old Valley Asylum appears. The light of the full moon gives the building an eerie glow.

"Are you going to be alright John? We can turn back if you want to."

He looks at Alison, "I pity the poor fool that gets in my way tonight." Immediately after saying this John begins to chatter his big teeth together like a skeleton in an old Disney cartoon. Alison grabs her flashlight then jumps out of the van.

"Come on John, let's get some good stuff then get the hell out of here." John grabs his camera and follows Alison over to the front gate.

"Wow look at those gothic creatures." John snaps a shot of the gargoyles.

"That would be enough to scare me sane." Alison grabs the gate and begins to climb the fence very slowly. She reaches the top in record time and looks around. "Wow I can see everything from here." As she scans the grounds she sees a small light that seems to be flickering inside the Asylum. "John, I think I see something inside the building. There may be a guard walking around inside, we have to be very sneaky."

John looks up to Alison, "Where is it?"

She points over to where the light is illuminating, "It looks like a light is turned on inside the Asylum, but it may be moving." She begins to ascend inside the gate. "Come on John let's get inside."

John begins to climb the fence; spitting in his hands just before he commences with the climb. He begins the climb and is about five feet up when his right hand slips; slicing his fingers on a rusty piece of iron protruding outward from the gate.

"Damn it all! Why am I doing this shit?" He reaches back up with both hands, now bleeding profusely, and pulls himself up again as blood begins to crawl down his arm. After about five more minutes of climbing John is finally able to pull his over-weight carcass to the top. "I need to get into shape Ally."

Alison looks up with concern, "How's your hand John?"

He smiles, "It's ok, I got another one anyway." In the distance the sound of a large canine howling at the moon penetrates their ears. The gate begins to slowly swerve from side to side; as much as the lock will allow it. John grabs the gargoyle perched on top, trying to keep his balance. "Ally I think I'm gonna fall, I feel like Humpty Dumpty!"

"Help!" John begins to slip again, this time he is sent ten feet to the ground. He lands feet first but the fall twists his ankle, John screams in agony, "Shit!" Alison sat there watching in terror as he fell, knowing she could do nothing. John grabs his ankle, "Oh shit, my ankle hurts like hell; it feels like I broke it. Great, I was supposed to go surfing next week in Malibu."

Alison rushes over to her fallen friend, "John, I'm so sorry, are you ok."

He grabs his ankle again, "What the hell happened to the gate?" The canine begins to howl again, this time with ferocious intensity.

"I don't know John, but let's get inside. It sounds like there's a wolf running around out here or something else." She grabs John and helps him to his feet. The two begin to walk toward the main entrance inside the gate. Two fountain pools of discolored water sit parallel to the entrance of the main hospital building. At one time they must have been beautiful sparkling pools of water but now they look as if death had visited them as well. The two reach the main door and sit on the porch to take a breather.

"John maybe you should stay here and rest. I can go inside by myself and look around. I have a flashlight."

John grabs her arm, "Ally I got a bad feeling about this one. Maybe we should just go. Is this story that important to you?" She kisses him on the forehead; "Yes it is John. I don't even know why, but I feel like it is?" The creature howls again in the distance but this time it feels much closer. John continues to tremble with fear. "Hurry Alison, please hurry. You don't want to see a grown man wet himself do you?"

Alison rises to her feet, takes a deep breath, then walks over to a broken window near the front door and climbs through the jagged entrance. The howling of the canine stops at the exact moment that Alison disappears into the dark Asylum. John sits outside near the fountain breathing very heavily, he hopes that Alison will soon crawl out of the building so they can leave this horrible place and never return again.

The cobwebs surrounded Alison like a nightmarish prison cell. It was completely dark inside the building; a small shaft of light extended from the broken window and created a circle around Alison's body. She reaches into her backpack and retrieves her flashlight. Alison stands to her feet and turns her small light on hoping to illuminate her situation.

"What was that?" The scampering of little feet can be heard all around her now. It was as if someone or something was circling her. She shines her flashlight all around the room but can see nothing except dark lifeless walls and spider webs. The sound of tiny shoes pounding against the hard floor continues; this time further in the distance it seems. In the corner of the room Alison spies a partially open door. She instinctively feels that she needs to get to that door.

"Time to get my story," Alison slowly creeps toward the open passage. She wished she had brought a machete for the thick forest of cobwebs; they seem to try to choke her, one web even slides into her mouth. She gags and spits it out onto the floor. Out of the corner of her eye she spots a gigantic spider a mere two feet away. It had to be at least twelve inches long. Alison hated spiders especially ones that were bigger then her head. This one seemed to have spotted her and was inching its way closer. When she was a small child Alison was bitten by a brown spider and almost died. Her heart began to pound frantically in her chest. Alison was about four feet away from the door now, about four feet too far she thought. She had to hold her breath now. Alison closes her eyes and leaps into the next room, her slight frame slides across the dirty floor finally coming to a stop. She stands up quickly shaking the webs from her face and hair.

Alison looks back into the room of the giant spider where it seems to have stopped at the door as if it were guarding the room from anyone trying to re-enter. It looked as if she was going to have to find another way out if she wanted to leave without becoming lunch for an enormous arachnid. The room she has entered appears to be a surgery room. She noticed a switch on the wall that beckoned her to pull it. Alison reaches over and tugs on the lever to come down but it seems to be stuck. The laughter of a child blows through the room like a cool breeze and echoes all around her. Alison's heart stops beating for a moment and then sharply begins to pump again, sending a burning sensation from her head to her beautifully manicured toes.

"Hello, who's there?" Alison grabs her flashlight and pulls a small knife out of her backpack. She had forgotten that it was there until now. She begins to search the room almost spinning around like a top, swinging the blade in a protective manner.

"John, is that you?" The lever on the wall that she had tried to pull earlier slowly is pushed down on its own by some unseen force. Alison sees this and slowly backs away from the switch. In a brilliant spark a large bulb above her head explodes sending shards of glass down upon her. She covers her face trying to avoid the sharp pieces of glass now raining down. Alison shakes her head like a wet dog trying to extract the broken pieces of glass from her hair. The sound of a crying child begins to penetrate her ears and her mind. Alison pulls herself back to her feet, confused more than ever now.

"Who is there?" Blood has begun to trickle down from her wrist. Alison examines her arm with her hand a long shallow cut has appeared. She rips a piece of cloth off from her shirt and wraps it around her wrist trying to stop the bleeding. She shines her flashlight in the direction of the crying child but she can see nothing but the entrance of what seems to be an office. Alison tries to pump herself up. "Keep going Ally. Don't give up now!"

She noticed that everything inside the building was left as it was that fateful day they closed the Asylum, it felt as if she was inside a time capsule, a very dark and scary time capsule. Alison slowly enters the office, trembling and bleeding more with every step. She had to mentally twist her own arm just to keep moving forward now.

She could even see a diploma on the wall which read, "Doctor Thomas Henderson. Class of 1948 I can't believe they left this here for so long." Alison walks around to the desk and begins to search the drawers for anything she could find. All the drawers were empty containing only dust and spider webs. Alison turns to leave the room when she notices the diploma on the wall is missing. She searches around the room almost stepping on it; she spies it lying on the floor behind the desk. She crawls under the desk to retrieve the document. Alison picks up the diploma carefully; a small piece of paper falls to the floor from behind the frame. "

What is this?" She opens the paper to reveal a small crusted note. Alison shines her light on the paper and begins to read it.

"My Dearest Samantha, I love you with all my heart. The first day I saw you when you started working here I knew that we would be together. For a time you made me forget about my loss. I am sorry for what has happened and for what must happen but it's the only way, it is what my brothers require. Our son will always be a secret to us. His life is a gift and a curse." Alison has made herself as comfortable as she can be for being crammed under the desk in such a tight spot. She is reading the letter like a young boy reads a comic book. The world has seemed to disappear around her. She pushes the note closer to her face and reads on. Alison was now lost in this past world.

"My love is forever and when I go I will still love you. It is hidden to the world but to us it is everything. If my wife were to find out about us it would kill her instantly. That is why I choose to keep it a secret. I know that is why you do not tell your husband as well." Alison continues to read on completely under the spell of this document. "My son is dead and they must pay for this. The new blood will bring back the old blood, they promised me this. It is my only chance to bring him back. You are the only thing that I do not hate about life anymore. When this is all over I hope you understand why I did it. Someone is coming I must..." Suddenly a loud howl can be heard coming from inside the Asylum. It was the same noise she had heard when she was outside with John. Alison is awoken from her trance and looks around the room frantically.

She tucks the note away in her pocket. Her arm is bleeding pretty badly and she knows she needs to get to a doctor soon. She spots a closed door on the right side of the room so Alison goes over to test the lock. The old door begins to open right before her eyes; she places her knife in stabbing mode ready for anything. The smell of burning flesh enters her nostrils. It reminds her of the stench from the prison and Alex Hoard. She begins to gag; trying to avoid losing her lunch. Alison shines her flashlight into the room, without warning a few bats whiz by her head missing her by mere inches. Alison ducks to avoid them dropping her flashlight in the process. The flashlight hits the ground, she can here the familiar sound of batteries scattering around the floor. The room is now completely basement black. She can see nothing! Alison drops to her knees and begins feeling around the floor hoping to find her flashlight and the batteries. The floor is damp and very dusty. Alison's fingers crawl around like cockroaches praying that she will find the batteries she dropped; at this point having any kind of light is all she can think about.

"Come on Ally find this flashlight and get out of here." Through her desperate search she luckily finds the flashlight and two batteries but she's unable to locate the third battery needed to get the flashlight to actually work! She continues to feel around the floor, when her hand crosses something that feels like a small shoe, she reaches higher, then she feels a small leg standing outside of her visual range Alison jumps back and lands on her rump roast. The voice of a young girl can be heard, "I see your soul." Two red glowing eyes appear, both of them about four feet above the ground. A "D" battery hurls threw the air hitting Alison right between the eyes. The creature lets out a demonic laugh and begins to slowly approach her. Alison backs into a wall and closes her eyes tightly; she is trapped like a caged animal. The demonic child slowly walks towards Alison arms outreached as if she wanted to give her a deadly hug. Alison lets out a loud cry, "No!" The creature stops moving forward and becomes completely silent again. Alison opens her eyes to see a long white candle levitating from the wall of darkness surrounding her. The candle begins to float over to her quivering body, stopping right in front of her fear covered face. Alison reaches over to grab the candle and as soon as she touches it the wick lights instantly. The four-foot figure lets out a howl of agony and runs into the darkness of the connecting room. The face was that of a small girl, she noticed it was riddled with holes and her eyes were as empty as the room she was in. This image was burnt into her mind when the mysterious candle illuminated the entire room for that split second.

Alison grabs the floating candle from mid air and holds it in front of her trembling body and with knees knocking she walks into the connecting room. The maze seemed to go on forever. The new chamber is filled with large glass windows each four to six feet in length and width. These large windows allow the moonlight to fill the cafeteria. She felt safer in this room because she could see so much more. Alison rests on a bench and tightens her cloth bandage.

"I need to find a way out of here soon." Rain was now hitting against the windows of the room, hard winds begin to shake them as well. Another thunderstorm has hit the city again. It was the fifth storm that month. She hoped that wherever John was, he was safe and very far from there.

Strangely the glow of the candle that had appeared from no where made her feel protected. She knew that someone had been looking out for her by scaring off the little creature she had encountered, someone that loved her. Just as she thought this the candle she was holding began to melt in her hands. She quickly drops the waxy object to the floor. Alison sits there and begins to think out loud, "I could use a bubble bath right now. Maybe some great sex too or chocolate!" She closes her eyes and pictures her glorious porcelain, extra super, rotating, jumbo wide, extreme power jet tub. It brings a brief smile to her bruised face. She can practically smell the bubbles now.

Suddenly a sharp pain grips her shoulder; she turns to see a man standing there. Alison screams and in an instinctive survival mode she kicks the man in the groin.

Oww!" The man screams. It was Bermuda shorts John; he had startled her once again. She hugs the big guy as a sea of calm and relief rushes over her entire body.

"John you scared me!" He drops to the floor and rolls in agony due to the swift kick to the mommy and daddy button. Slowly John is able to get back to his feet.

"Sorry Ally, I just had to come in, that howling dog outside made me kind of scared. Now I wish I would have stayed outside!"

"We need to get out of here fast; we are both bleeding pretty bad."

John points to a small door in the corner of the cafeteria, "I think we can get out that way I think it leads to the back." The two make their way over to the door, Alison grabs the handle and is about to turn it when she hears a strange voice coming from outside the Asylum. She recognizes the voice quickly it is the voice of her friend John.

"Alison where are you?" She freezes in terror realizing that either John has a twin brother or the man behind her is not who he appears to be. She slowly pulls her knife from her pocket and in a fierce swing she spins around to see that no one is behind her. She is utterly alone.

The voice of John can be heard in the distance once more. "Alison where are you?" He yells louder, "Alison yell to me if you can hear me."

She replies at the top of her lungs, "I'm in here John, I'm in here." The pitter-patter of rain seems to be putting Alison in an almost trance-like state. Her entire life has changed in the last week. She was frightened that she might be going insane. A strong feeling seems to have been pushing her to continue on no matter what has happened. She didn't believe in ghosts or monsters as a child but now she had not only believed in them but she had seen them and she had felt them. It was swallowing her whole, this strange world she had entered into.

"CRASH!" A window shatters into a million pieces; torrential rain has begun to fall into the room forming a small river down the middle of the cafeteria. From the hole in the window a voice begins to permeate into the room.

"Alison, Alison, remove him." She pulls the door in the corner of the cafeteria open and falls into the water soaked grass of the courtyard. She had found a door that lead outside. The blood from her arm has begun to flow into the grass turning it bright red, the grass seemed to enjoy this and drink her life fluid. Alison tries to scramble to her feet and notices that four tombstones surround her now. Her feet begin to sink into the thick greedy mud ground. Her heart is pounding and ready to burst once more.

Alison begins frantically grabbing at anything she can trying to regain her balance. In the distance she can see what looks like forty or fifty small children wearing straight jackets and standing in a single file line, they all seem to be fixated on Alison's struggle. The rain is causing the skin on these children to slowly be washed off their skeleton frames as if it was pure acid. They neither moved nor spoke only watched intently as if waiting for something. She tries desperately to pull her leg from the mud but cannot retrieve them completely. It felt like quick sand. It was pulling her under

In her mind Alison can hear a tiny voice speaking to her, "So close now Alison. So close now. Release, Release." Alison sees a bright encompassing white flash; the hairs on her arms begin to stand up. She hears a loud crackle then her heartbeat and then nothing.

# Seven

As Star gets into her father's car she looks back towards her house to see her little puppy sniffs wagging his tail and smiling at her through the window. She didn't want to go to summer camp, especially one where every kid going was a major spoiled brat. Except her of course! As her father closed the door to the automobile she frowned with disgust hoping he would notice her unkind gesture. She was the only child born from two baby-boomer parents. Star had felt alone her entire life; she wasn't the most outgoing person. She had a hard time making friends especially because she was used to moving every six months. Her father was a "big-wig" oil-guy and personal friend of the one and only Tyler Hoffman. This summer the parental-units were going to Switzerland and then Australia and then who knows where else. She was going to the world's most expensive baby-sitter. She slid her headphones on and cranked up her Heavy Metal as loud as her machine would play. She sunk back into her leather seat and drifted off, but not before she screamed out loud that her entire family could "Suck it!" It was off to summer camp and her parents couldn't be more pleased. Star was a good girl she was just misunderstood and very vocal about her feelings. Star had been kicked out of her last three schools. It was hard for her to play nice as they say. Star faded into her sleep world as her father tore down the interstate towards the "Valley-Super-Summer-Camp." She did not know it yet but things were about to take a very dark turn. At this moment there really was bliss in ignorance.

As Allen got out of the limo he looked around, "This place looks like crap to me." A large man wearing a navy blue suit and matching tie exits the other limo door.

"Now son, it's imperative to me that you behave yourself this summer. I am trying to get reelected next year and I don't need any tabloid stories to ruin my chances, your mother was enough of an embarrassment with her drinking problem. So be a good boy or else it's off to military school in the Arctic Circle with your brother!" Allen turns his attention back to the limo where a 400 pound man eating a Bacon Cheeseburger and a pudding pop stares back at him. It was Teddy his brother, that poor bastard didn't even know what was coming; his fat ass was two days away from being shipped off to the home of the Polar Bear and icebergs. Allen shook his head in disgust. "Bye Teddy Bear!" Teddy waved his arm at Allen mayo and lettuce flying everywhere. Allen closes his eyes and takes a deep breath. "Ok Allen, turn and walk away." Allen turns as his father speeds away in the mayo covered limo. In the distance he could here the loud cry of 400 pound Teddy. "I guess he finished his burger," Allen thought. He was finally free of his oppressors.

The young man picks up his duffle bag and guitar from the ground where it had been tossed by his father. Allen was your typical musician type: long hair, tattoos, goatee and over-sized six string; he was nothing like his father and he liked it that way.

In a few seconds Allen reaches the Camp facility registration table where an old frizzy haired woman was sitting, she was signing up unhappy campers one by one. Allen was one of the final campers to arrive so he headed to the back of the seventy-person line. As he reached the back of the line he dropped his heavy duffel on the ground. Allen pulled a ciggy from his jacket and felt around his pocket for a lighter.

"Dammit, all I want is to smoke a cigarette and I have no fucking lighter!" A young girl in front of him turns around and raises a lighter to his lips. She blazes his cancer-stick then turns back around without saying a word.

Allen takes a puff then taps this mysterious girl on the shoulder, "Um, excuse me." She turns her head to face him. "Hey I'm Allen."

She replies softly, "I'm Star."

Allen pulls a quick drag of his nicotine, "That's a cool name, Star."

She smiles, "Thanks, parents, hippies." The two laugh.

"I have a question for you Star, if you don't smoke then why are you carrying this lighter around?"

She leans over places her lips centimeters from his ears, "It's not mine; I just boosted it from the guy in front of me in line. I got his wallet to but apparently he's on welfare 'cause no cash was found." Allen bursts forth with obnoxious laughter mixed with snorting. The line in its entirety turns to see what the commotion is all about. The two decide to park it on the grass fearing that the line will never move.

"So what do your folks do Star?"

"My dad is into making money and abandoning his family so when he has time to take a vacation he drops me off at various youth prisons about ten times a year. Star looks around the facility, "I guess since this place is for rich kids he thought it would be good for me to be completely surrounded by other kids who are ignored by there parents and treated like shit." Star continues to scan her surroundings, "This place is creepy."

Allen smirks, "Wow, you finished, sounds like you are carrying around some heavy baggage Star." Star reaches over and pulls a cig from Allen's pocket. "Hey I thought you didn't smoke?" Star lights the cigarette with her newly acquired lighter.

"I do now." Star takes a drag, trying not to cough, "So tell me about your family Allen. Let me guess your father's in the oil industry or something."

"They're all dead, well except my stepfather. He's an asshole."

"Oh I'm so sorry Allen." He places his hand over his eyes to cover up the tears. "That's ok; the worst part is how they died." Star places her hand on his knee. "They were all killed in a bowling accident; there were arms, and legs and pins flying everywhere. I did get a strike though." Allen smiles wide from ear to ear.

Star punches him in the arm, so Allen, in retaliation, pounces on the girl wrestling her to the ground. Star struggles to escape his grip but to no avail. Allen releases her but she remains underneath him not trying to move away. Star reaches up and grabs Allen by the shirt pulling him back down on top of her and kisses him passionately. Allen is almost shocked to death by this aggressive move. He falls over on the grass as if he was just knocked out by a heavyweight uppercut. Star laughs and runs from the line towards the newly renovated camper bunkhouses.

Allen shakes his head, "That girl is crazy, I think I love her!" A large boot appears in front of young Allen Worthy III, he looks up to see a mountain of a man, or in this case, a mountain of a boy standing there. Allen thought he looked like a cross between the Fonz and Curly of the stooges, only a seven-foot version.

"Hey lover boy, I saw you playing tonsil hockey with my ex-girlfriend Star." Allen swallows a rock. "Nobody kisses her except for me. Especially no gay boy like you!"

"Uh, uh." The Sasquatch grabs Allen by the collar lifting him off of the ground. "Listen very closely, if you want to live to see another sunrise I suggest you stay away from her. Keep your boner in your pocket, she's mine queer!"

Allen in an almost instinctive survival mode kicks the gorilla man in the family jewels. The behemoth drops Allen to the ground and falls over in agony. Like a wounded dragon the jealous ex-lover rises back to his feet, fire ready to burst forth from his mouth, he pounds his fist as he slowly walks towards Allen. "You are dead meat!"

"That's enough, Max I'm not your girlfriend anymore. Leave us alone." The look of anger on Max's face turns to an expression that you would expect to see on a lost Puppy's face as he sees Star run to Allen's defense and not to his.

"But, but, I thought we still had a chance. I thought you loved my guns?"

Star walks up to the giant, like Jack approaching the beanstalk, "Listen Max what don't you get, we are through, period end of story, bu-bye!" And with that the confrontation ends. Max gives Allen one more evil eye but then he lumbers off sulking all the way. Allen rubs his neck trying to understand what just happened.

"Jeez, Star when did you start working with endangered mountain gorillas?"

Star chuckles, "Oh that was one mistake I wish I never would have made. Max's father and my pops worked together, well, my dad thought it would be good if we dated, ya know rich marrying the rich kinda thing." Star walks over to Allen and gives him another kiss on the cheek and the two walk back to the line hand in hand.

About two hours later they finally reach the front of the line where they receive their room assignments and summer fun packets, complete with the schedule of events.

Allen walks Star to her dormitory and this time gives her a kiss on the lips, "I'll see you tonight at the welcome pep-rally." The butterflies in their stomachs begin to flutter all around them now. Love or lust is definitely in the air.

Star hugs him in return, "Ya know I never thought I would meet someone as cool as you, especially in a place like this." She hugs him again and enters the building. As soon as she is out of sight Allen begins jumping up and down singing and yelling all the way back to the male dorm hall.

" Oh Star you are by far: faster than my car; you get me drunker then a bar, hide that passion like a jar and make me wetter then some tar, oh Star." Allen has never been in love before but he thinks that is all about to change very soon.

Allen enters the male dormitory and heads to the fourth floor where his room is located. The newly redesigned buildings had the interior feel of a log cabin; the wood paneling covered everything that wasn't nailed down. The long narrow hallways were furnished with thick red carpeting and velvet framed paintings. Each room consisted of two beds, two desks, a small TV, a VCR and two closets. "My dad paid $50,000 to send me here? It looks like a 70s bordello!" After what felt like an eternity Allen finally reaches his room. He notices that the door is shut so he gives it a light tap, without warning a skinny hand reaches through the door pulling him into the room. The door slams behind him and Allen is sent flying onto one of the beds. Once Allen regains his focus he is shocked to see a tall skinny, Mohawk sporting punk reject standing over him.

The Sid Vicious wannabe points his finger at Allen, "Don't ever enter my room without knocking!" Allen, now enraged by this freaky boy's threat, jumps to his feet and pushes the punk against the wall, pinning him next to the closed door.

"First of all if you were listening I did knock and second of all what the hell are you doing in my room?" Allen squeezes the boy tightly against the wall.

Mohawk boy reaches out his long hand in a greeting gesture, "I'm Goob, but my friends call me the King of Hardcore." Allen shakes his head and releases his death grip on this "Goober".

"I'm Allen your roommate, I guess." The skinny Goob fixes his collar and cracks his neck while bouncing up and down on his toes, apparently inspired by a TY-BO video or something.

The two exchange a very awkward greeting. Allen grabs his duffel bag and begins to unpack his belongings and place them in the drawers provided. Goob grabs two dirty trash bags full of his very smelly things and throws them onto the bed nearest the window. A few sardines fall to the floor as well. The smell fills the tiny room.

"I need the bed closest to the window, I get claustrophobic."

Allen smiles and thinks to himself, "Maybe he wants that bed because that hair takes up all his breathing space, or maybe it helps keep his BO from lingering inside the bedroom." Goob pulls out a very stinky cigar and lights it up, while Allen finishes unpacking; he gives himself a grand tour of their tiny cell, which will be home for the next three months. Allen walks over to the sink and begins to shave off his scruffy goatee.

"So Goob, how did you get thrown in here with the rest of us?" Goob is about to answer when he hears footsteps walking down the hall, he quickly dumps the cigar into the sink nearly burning Allen. There is a knock at the door and then a voice is heard.

"Make sure that you are at the meeting in the entertainment complex tonight it's mandatory, so be there. Check your campus map to find out where it is." With this statement the unseen man can be heard walking down the hall to the next room.

"Man, I thought you had to commit a crime to be thrown in prison."

Allen laughs, "I know, we have to be drug tested every week."

Goob swallows "Gulp, really? Allen could you pee in my cup for me?"

Allen begins to whisper, "They even give random enemas."

Goob places his hands over his anus, "That's an exit not an entrance man!"

Allen rolls over with laughter. "Got ya Goob!" Allen continues to howl with amusement. He smacks Goob on the back as the paranoid boy squirms with disapproval.

"You bastard, you lying sack of shit!" Goob can't hold it in any longer, he too begins to laugh. "Ok, you got me, I owe you one dude!"

While laughing Allen thinks to himself, "Goob may be strange, bordering on psycho, but I think he's a good guy, I just need to get him to shower once in awhile" Thinking even deeper though; he was pondering becoming closer with another person, that person was his new love, Star. He thought that this summer may actually turn out to be a good one after all. It's the beginning of another great summer of love, one that will be hard to forget but even harder to survive.

The entertainment complex was a completely new building, built on the site of one of the old demolished patient wards. The youth were now congregating inside this massive hall. A large stage was erected in front of the already gigantic crowd. Star pushes her way through the crowd screaming out for Allen.

"Star, over here." Star turns her head spotting Allen sitting on the shoulders of a giant beanpole with a Mohawk. Star makes her way toward this curious two-headed monster. Allen jumps down from Goob's shoulders nearly face-planting on the floor.

"Hey Star, this is my roommate Goob." Star shakes his long alien looking hand.

"Hi Goob, I'm Star." Goob smiles but then becomes very distracted with a young girl wearing all black standing directly behind Star.

He clears his throat, "Who is that?"

Star turns to the mystery girl, "Oh, this is my roommate Xona." Goob pushes Allen and Star to the side and reaches out grabbing Xona's hand. He gently kisses her tiny fingers.

"Hello beautiful, I'm Goob; you can call me the king of hardcore." Xona pulls her hand from his grip and places an accurate karate kick to the back of Goob's head sending him flying into the surrounding crowd.

She smiles, "You can call me the Queen bee." Goob stands back up rubbing his sore melon and looks into Xona's eyes.

"Wow I think I'm in love." The sound of major back-feed can be heard coming from one of the stage mikes.

"Good evening campers and welcome to the best summer of your very short lives." The screaming of the assembled crowd now ceases as they all focus on the greasy looking man who has taken center stage. "I'm Tyler Hoffman, the man behind the dream, the very dream that allowed all of you to be here today."

Star leans over to Allen and whispers, "More like the nightmare."

Tyler walks to the edge of the stage as if he were going to take a dive, "Children look at your neighbor because by the end of the summer he or she may become your new best friend." Goob slides his frail frame next to where Xona is standing.

She gives him the evil eye, "Or your worst enemy!" Goob smiles in response.

"I know you hate me but standing next to you is good enough for me."

Tyler begins to speak about his great life accomplishments as most dictators do. "I want to make one thing clear with all of you; your parents have given us the utmost authority in dealing with any bad behavior that any of you may exhibit. I do hope that that won't be necessary." The campers have now become completely silent at this stark announcement. "I expect everyone to be on there best behavior and to follow all rules including lights out at 10:00 p.m." Tyler wrings his hands and smiles sarcastically.

Star, who has tuned out most of what Tyler has said since he stepped onstage, has begun to peer around her surroundings. Teenagers from punk to prep surround her. She wonders how she got here to begin with, like tiny fingers on her spine she begins to shiver with chills. Allen who has been staring at Star this entire speech places his arm around her and squeezes her closer to him.

"Star, are you feeling alright?" Star has started to turn pale white.

Star turns to Allen and as if she were in a trance and responds, "Huh, What, I feel weird Allen." Star closes her eyes squeezing them tight with agony.

Allen places his hand on her forehead. "Star you're burning up." Star feels another surge of ice cover her entire body causing her already unsteady legs to finally give out. Allen catches the sick girl inches from the hard floor. "Star, Star, what's wrong?" The crowd around the two begins to spread out giving the sick girl space.

Tyler sees the commotion from atop the stage; he covers the mic with one hand and begins to bark orders to another man standing nearby; "Go take care of what ever needs to be taken care of over there, that's why I pay you bastards." The burly man reacts instantly rushing toward the unconscious girl, pushing kids to the floor along the way.

"What happened to her?" The man pushes Goob to the floor, "Move punk."

Allen shakes his head in disbelief, "I don't know she just passed out." The man grabs the young girl and heads toward the exit of the complex; Allen follows her closely.

A second man looking much like a club bouncer places his hand on Allen's chest, "That's far enough lover boy; you can't follow her all the way." Allen struggles but cannot get by the human wall.

Allen now frustrated, "You don't understand, she's my friend."

The giant man smiles, "She'll be just fine." The man carrying Star passes through a side door taking the young girl out of sight. Allen returns to Goob, "Where are they taking her?" He continues to pace, meanwhile, Tyler has taken the stage again and continues with his presentation. "Have no fear children, now where were we?" All of a sudden Allen felt like a caged animal. He was worried sick about Star and wanted to see her. He knew something was terribly wrong and this feeling burnt in his gut.

As Star looked over the golden horizon a bright sun burnt its impression onto the fields of the green land. Where was she, and how did she get there? She saw some children playing in this mystical land, most of them running to and fro. Star stood there watching as the tall green grass blew in the breeze creating a green wave affect all around her. The landscape was beautiful. A crystal clear stream of cool water ran through her toes as she stood an inch deep in the long winding stream. On either side of the water Star sees a thick black forest that appeared to grow rapidly right in front of her and it even began to block out the rays of the sun. Star swivels her head on her shoulders trying to take in all that surrounds her. This was a strange disturbing feeling and it frightened her.

Star looked into the water below her as it began to increase in depth, right before her very eyes. Within thirty seconds the water level had risen to her waist. She struggles to walk toward the side of the stream, but it seems that as the stream increases in depth it also increases is width. The depth increases to the point where Star must begin to swim to reach the other side. With a sharp tug to her leg she is instantly brought beneath the frigid water. Star kicks, shakes and thrashes to be released from this icy grip. She turns her body in a complete circle; upon completion she is startled to see the face of an old man. White hair covers this disfigured corpse that seems to have been resting on the floor of this stream for what appears like decades. This figure is wearing an old tattered doctor's jacket. The decayed man squirms in a tormented way writhing in pain and eternal agony.

As Star struggles to be released from this force she hears the blood curdling voice of this old man, "Stay with me." With these final words the evil creature releases its grip allowing the girl to escape her near drowning. Star shoots to the surface gasping for air. She begins to scream for help but receives no response. She once again heads for the safety of dry land practicing her best impersonation of Mark Spitz. The white fingers resurface underneath Star's ankle grabbing her once more.

The face of the monster reemerges, "Come with me, I will take you home with me." Star screams and instinctively kicks the man in the face cracking his skull in multiple areas. The soggy brains begin to ooze from the man's cracked features. The complete bony corpse floats to the surface and starts to rub against Star's leg; she can feel every bony protrusion now. Star continues to scream, but even with this split skull the creature does not release his hold on her. He pulls her face close to his own opening his mouth, or what's left of it, as wide as possible. He begins to ram her into his broken mandible trying to swallow her whole. She screams in absolute horror.

Just as it seems that there is no hope for Star a bright blue light illuminates the waters icy depths and like a rocket thrust Star is propelled from the stream and is sent flying through the air to the dry earth nearby. Star somehow gets to her feet and peers into the water, there is no sign of the decrepit creature anymore, only a woman floating on her back, as if she is sleeping. The clear water has turned blood red. Star feels a tug on her shirt a small hand appears around her waist. Star cries out, "Help!" A second voice can be heard, a much younger voice. It is the voice of a small child.

"Don't leave us." The small boy touches Star on the leg.

Star pushes the small child away, "Who are you? What do you want from me?"

The little boy giggles, "Help us." The little boy points to a group of graves near the Asylum in the distance. Star looks in the direction to which the little child has pointed, she turns to ask another question but he has vanished. In the wind Star can hear the little boy's voice echoing, "Help us escape."

A bright light fills her face so Star covers her eyes to protect them. The light begins to fade slowly so she uncovers her face; she is startled once more to realize that she is sitting on a bed in what appears to be a clinic. A man wearing a white coat hovers over her; he begins to feel her forehead and then checks his clipboard. Star is startled by the man and gasps deeply. She pulls back from his cold touch.

"Relax, I'm Doctor Henderson." Star rubs her eyes, "What happened?" The doctor shakes his head, "Well young lady we are glad that you made it back, you seemed to have some sort of a seizure but your fine now."

Star quickly responds, "A man was trying to kill me, but this little boy saved me, he pulled me from the water and." Dr. Henderson has heard enough of her visions so he places his finger on Star's lips, "Shh, you need some rest, you are hysterical now." Star struggles to stand, but is stopped by the doctor, "Nurse get in her, I need a sedative." The doctor holds Star to the bed using his body weight to keep her still. The nurse quickly injects the sleeping agent into Star's arm. Within minutes Star has fallen into this drug-induced sleep.

Across the courtyard Allen lie awake in his bed wondering what had become of Star and more importantly how could he get to her. He had to do something to help her.

"Goob, I'm scared that something bad happened to her!"

Goob peers through the blinds into the courtyard, "Those bastards probably are having their way with her right now!"

Allen responds sharply, "Shut your mouth, don't say that!"

Goob turns his head towards Allen, "Geez I was joking. Man, I think you love her or something." Goob stands up and walks to the window to look outside.

Allen sits up from his reclined position, "I have to go find her."

Goob quickly closes the blinds completely, "You must be crazy, and did you see those big thugs that Tyler has patrolling this place? They look like pro-wrestlers, steroids and all." Goob opens the door to peer into the hall as if someone were listening.

Allen responds, "I don't care, I'm worried about her." Goob quickly shuts the door. He walks over to Allen and places his hand on his shoulder.

Goob smiles, "It would be fun to break curfew the first night! You talked me into it, what do we do?" Allen rubs his eyes and begins to come up with a plan to find Star.

# Eight

John sat there and cried over the comatose body. Alison lay there in the hospital bed motionless since the incident at the old Asylum almost two months earlier. The night the two ventured out Alison had been struck by lightning. John found her body limp and lifeless lying over the grave of some forgotten soul. He had rushed her to his van and then to the Valley Hospital where she has stayed in her near death state to the present day.

John caresses Alison's arm speaking softy to her, "Oh Ally, I'm so sorry for what happened. I had such a bad feeling about being there. I had no choice." The giant teddy bear continues to weep. "Come back to us Ally, come back." A knock is heard at the door, John turns his head to see Alison's mother standing there with her arms crossed and a very serious look on her face. John rises to his feet and walks over to Mrs. O'Connell to give her a hug. To his surprise he receives a half-hearted response.

"John why were you two snooping around that retched old place? Why didn't you try to talk her out of going there?" John remains silent.

Mrs. O'Connell turns her face to Alison, "Maybe you should leave now John. I want to be alone with my baby."

John grabs his things and with head down slowly walks towards the exit, when he reaches the door he turns toward Alison's tear covered mother, "I'm sorry. You know why." John slowly closes the door behind him. Mrs. O'Connell sits down next to her daughter and pulls out a very dusty old book containing even older fairy tales.

"Alison I know that you can hear me baby. I've got your old fairy tales book; I'm going to read your favorite story sweetheart." She opens the book and begins to read, "Once upon a time there was a young peasant girl who lived in the forest."

As she begins to weave the fairy tale a loud thump emanates from the closet in the corner of the hospital room. Mrs. O'Connell is very startled; she places the book on the floor and begins to walk towards the strange noise. She reaches out to open the closet door when she hears it again, this time it's twice as loud. Mrs. O'Connell swallows hardly. She swiftly flings open the door but finds nothing but pure black space. She notices that the closet is extremely cold but it's completely empty. She closes the door and returns to her place by Alison's side.

Mrs. O'Connell opens the fairy tale and returns to the magical place she was moments earlier, still weary of the strange noise coming from the closet.

"Now this was a very special girl, some said she possessed magic powers."

A small drop of red fluid falls from the ceiling and splatters on the pages of the old book sending Mrs. O'Connell into a panic. She quickly throws her head back to see her daughter, to her amazement, floating above her, blood leaking from her nose and mouth. Mrs. O'Connell is now in a shocked motionless state as she watches the floating body. There were scratching noises now emanating for all four walls of the room as if a witch were clawing her way out of a claustrophobic grave. It was terrifying.

The face of Alison turned pale white, the eyes black as night death. Alison's mouth opens as if forced to do so, "Secrets will rise; time is short. I wait for you. I wait for you my love."

She screams again in terror at this horrific sight, the voice that came from Alison was not her own but that of a man, a man Mrs. O'Connell knew very well. Like a rock dropped from a 747 Alison comes crashing down onto her bed cracking the frame in half. Mrs. O'Connell continues to scream and cry out for help. The jolt of the descent seems to awaken the possessed woman; she squirms around in her bed trying to make sense of where she is and what has happened to her. Mrs. O'Connell grabs Alison and gives her a tearful squeeze. The roller coaster of emotions is too much for her soul.

"Oh Alison you are back. No one will ever take you away from me again." Alison, still in a semi-vegetable state replies to her mother, "Mom, what happened?" Alison coughs and begins to experience dry heaves. "I saw a man killing these children he was a doctor." After hearing this, her mothers face changes from joy to terror. The words have touched a nerve deep in her heart, and deep in her soul.

"That man is dead, he can't hurt you now." Mrs. O'Connell begins to cry.

A hospital security guard finally enters the room huffing and puffing as if he just finished the Boston Marathon, "Is everything alright?" A powdered doughnut falls from his hand to the floor. "Oh my God, what happened here?"

Mrs. O'Connell answers the man, "My daughter just came out of her coma get a doctor quickly." The overweight man runs out of the room and searches for the closest doctor.

Alison tugs on her mother's shirt, "Mom who is that man? You know something."

Mrs. O'Connell clears her throat then begins to tell her daughter another type of story, "He is a man I met a long time ago, and his name is Thomas Henderson."

"Mom you actually knew this man?" Alison shakes her head in disbelief.

Mrs. O'Connell looks away from her daughter, "Honey I don't know if you are ready for what I have to tell you." She takes Alison by the hand. "The truth is…"

Before she can finish her sentence two doctors come barreling through the door. The men were no doubt in shock to see this brain-dead vegetable sitting up and talking as if she had just woken up from a nap. She had beaten the odds and regained consciousness. She had come back to the land of the living. Quickly the entire medical staff surrounds Alison's bed; her mother is rudely pushed to the side. Mrs. O'Connell was filled with every emotion possible, fear after seeing her daughter become possessed by something evil, joy after seeing her come back to life from the coma and agony because she was about to reveal something so shocking that she wasn't sure how Alison would take it. Telling her daughter the truth is what scared her the most.

# Nine

Allen slowly opened his bedroom door as he checked the halls for signs of life.

"Alright Goob I think I can sneak out, I don't see anybody."

Goob peers through the blinds of their window, "The grounds look clear too." Allen takes a deep breath, then like a ninja slides down the hall. He narrowly avoids being picked up by the rotating hall camera. He is on a quest to find Star. Allen tiptoes quickly down the hall until he reaches the stairs that lead to the exit on the first floor.

"Who's there?" Allen turns around to see a security guard waving a flashlight towards him; the guard is trying to see who is attempting to break curfew on the very first night. Curfew meant stay in your bed to Tyler Hoffman!

"I'm toast," he thought, as he threw open the door and ran down the stairs. The security guard carrying about an extra two hundred pounds around his waist huffed his way down the hall trying to keep up with the young man. Allen's heart was pounding and his face was tomato red, his sweat streamed down his face as he flew down the stairs. When he reached the bottom floor Allen noticed another guard standing outside listening to his walky-talky, no doubt talking to chubby guard up stairs. He was positioned outside the front door waiting to ambush Allen when he bolted into the night. Allen stood there trying to think of another way to get past these goons. He had to do it quick!

He notices an open door next to the entrance leading into a large supplies closet, Allen dives headfirst into this room narrowly escaping the fat man who has finally reached the bottom of the staircase behind him. Allen covers his mouth trying to cover up his heavy breathing. His heart was racing like the number seven horse in the last race.

The fat guard calls guard number two on his walky-talky, "Joe I lost him, I have no sign of him. Maybe I'm just seeing things; my wife said that Viagra could have massive side effects. I'm heading upstairs to check again just in case." He turns back to head up the stairs wishing the building was equipped with an elevator when he hears a sneeze emanate from the closet. His large ears perk up as he swivels his head toward Allen's hiding place. Allen was toast; his goose was cooked for sure.

A large grin covers his face, "Well, well, well, it's seems like a little mouse has a cold." He begins to approach the door, Allen is now aware that he's about to be caught. He frantically looks around the closet for somewhere to hide or something to bash him with. He spies a mop so he grabs it tightly ready to hit a home run.

"Look at me, look at me!" The guard is stunned to see a tall skinny naked Mohawk boy run right by him. "You can't catch me fat ass!"

"What the hell?" Goob heads toward the front door, the fat Hoffman goon gives chase and is shortly assisted by the guard hiding outside the door. The two men can hardly keep up with Goob who on this night looks like a streaking track star and a night gazelle. Allen pops his head out of the closet and checks to see if the coast is clear. He flees out the back door instead of the front where Goob is running in circles like a chicken with his head cut off. Allen can't help but smile at this Jerry Springer spectacle.

"I owe that weirdo one big time," he thinks to himself as he heads towards the tower hospital prison where Star is being held. The main tower looks like an old lighthouse mixed with a medieval torture chamber. Allen is able to sneak past another guard who is sleeping outside the main building, the boy heads toward the clinic entrance, following the trail of sleeping security guards like bread crumbs. When Allen reaches the nurse's office he can see the young girl passed out on her bed. In the adjoining room Allen barely notices a nurse sitting at a table drinking a cup of coffee and trying to figure out her crossword puzzle. Allen drops to the floor out of view just as she looks up after hearing the squeak of Allen's new Adidas. She scans the room sees that all is well and then returns to trying to find a four letter word for shrubbery. Allen has to figure out how he can get past her, then it hits him, slip her a sleeping pill from the Pharmacy room in her coffee somehow. A crazy plan, but so crazy it just might work. He crawls on his stomach until he reaches the Pharmacy down the hall. Allen tugs on the door knob but it's locked. Can anything else go wrong today?

"Shit, what do I do now?" Allen barely notices a security officer approaching; he looks around in a panic for a place to hide and sees a large trash receptacle nearby so without delay he leaps into the can amercing his entire body in the refuse. Allen can hear as the guard calls out to the young nurse. She quickly comes running down the hall towards the man, like a puppy answering a master's call.

Allen begins to hear something that sounds like kissing, dirty wet kissing! He wondered how long these two lovebirds would stay there. Then he hears the door to one of the patient's rooms swing open and the sound of pants unzipping. This could be his only chance to slide past them.

Allen hears the door lock, "Hopefully he's not a twenty second guy."

Allen jumps out of the trash and runs back into Star's hospital room. He leans over her bed and kisses her on the forehead. His face covered in worry as he views her limp body. He could tell she was heavily sedated at this point.

Allen begins to speak to her in a soft and comforting voice, "I'm glad you're ok Star." The roll of thunder of the approaching storm outside can be heard coming from the clouds now forming above. The storm was beginning to roll in now in more ways than one. A strange energy permeated the entire atmosphere making the air thick as smoke.

Allen is filled with relief though to see his love still alive, "It was all worth it," he thought to himself. A sharp pinching sensation suddenly runs through his arm, Allen looks down to see Star's hand gripping him as if she were in a struggle for her very life. Star's face is covered in a mask of fear, grinding her teeth, eyes still locked shut. She begins to mumble incoherently as if she were being strangled slowly. Allen grabs her frail body and begins to rock her vigorously.

. "Star wake up, wake up!" She gasps for air finally opening her eyes.

"Allen, Allen!"

He pulls the frightened girl to his chest, "I'm here Star everything is ok now, even though getting here was a bitch." She pulls the boy closer to her squeezing the life out of him. "I feel so sleepy Allen." She points to her right arm, "This doctor gave me something in my arm, it still burns like fire ants crawling in my skin."

Allen grabs her tightly, "What's going on Star?"

"It's this place Allen, we shouldn't be here!" Her voice intensifying with every word, "We have to leave now!" After barely completing her sentence six men enter the room, among the men are Dr. Henderson and Mr. Hoffman.

"You weren't planning on leaving us, were you?" Tyler walks over to the two frightened youth, "Your parents left you here because they didn't want you, so now I am in charge of dealing with you in an appropriate fashion."

Allen rises to his feet, "I don't care what our parents said, you can't keep us here against our will, and we're going home right now." Allen clinches his fists, ready to fight.

Tyler smiles a devilish smile then grabs Allen by the collar, "Now listen here boy; you will do exactly as I tell you to do. You are my boy now!" He grips the boy's collar tighter, "Do you understand me?" Tyler releases the boy, who was now dangling in mid air, sending him falling to the floor. "Think of this place as your new home. A new beginning and an ending!" Tyler points to one of his men "Take him back to his room and stay outside his door all night." The big gorilla grabs Allen and carries him out of the room. Star clinches her fist; she hurls it towards Tyler Hoffman belting him right on the nose.

Tyler grabs her hand and pushes her back onto the bed, "That wasn't very nice, but don't worry because what I have planned for all of you is very nice." The crazed man begins to laugh, "Especially for you my dear." Tyler disgustingly tongues the girl on the cheek, "Tomorrow is a big day, there are baskets to weave and horses to ride and who knows what else." Tyler raises his eyebrows as if he had heard a strange noise; he quickly bolts out of the room, his men following in single file. At this point Star wasn't sure which was scarier, this place or Tyler Hoffman. Dr. Henderson straps her back to the bed and with another quick pinch Star slips deep into unconsciousness once again.

# Ten

It was nearly four in the morning as Mrs. O'Connell and Alison pulled up to her apartment building. Mrs. O'Connell was visibly shaken; she felt a large lump enter her throat. The weight of the world was dropped onto her shoulders. The truth had to come out about her past. It was a past that she had tried to forget and one that she had never wanted to share with her beloved daughter Alison. This past had now come back to haunt her. The past was alive and well and it was looking for revenge.

Alison slid her key into the front door and turned the knob slowly, as she entered her home she began to speak to her mother, "Mom everything is so strange right now."

"I feel as if my whole world has been turned on its side." Mrs. O'Connell places her hand on Alison's shoulder and assists Alison as they walk into her bedroom. Alison slowly crawls into her bed, her mother covering her with thick blankets.

"Sweetie before I tell you something I just want you to know that I love you with all of my heart and your father loved you with all his heart. I would never let any harm come to you." She grabs Alison's hand; "A long time ago I was once a nurse at the old Valley Asylum. When I worked there I met a young doctor. It was truly love at first sight. His name was Thomas Henderson." She clears her throat, trying not to cry, "Well, we got to know each other over some time working together. The story has turned into a complete vivid flashback for her mother. I made the biggest mistake of my life and I..." The emotion has become too much for her causing her to weep like a flooding river. "I'm so sorry Alison. I had an affair with him." Alison stares at the ceiling of her bedroom shocked; her jaw dropping to her chest. Her only comfort was the lick of her puppy at her big toe. Mrs. O'Connell continues revealing her dark secret, "Your older brother Jeremy was only your half brother. Dr. Henderson was his real father." Shock and anger begin to fill her veins as her mother continues.

"Why would you do it mom? Wasn't dad good enough for you?" Alison covers her face with her hands. The anger and rage began to fill her vessel as she listened.

"I was young and foolish Alison. Please forgive me, but I have to tell you everything Sweetie, that's not all. I also did something else. I was so easily manipulated at that age." Mrs. O'Connell lifts up her left foot exposing a small tattoo on the bottom of it. Alison turns her head away in complete disbelief.

"Look, please." Alison had never noticed it before. It was a lightning bolt. "Can you see it? It's a mark of shame; I was in a cult called B.E. for short. I am so ashamed of what they did." She lowers her leg to the floor, "I was only at a low level of the group we took drugs and played with Ouija boards and stupid stuff like that. Our leader was convinced he was the future ruler of the world. He was all about blood for blood and just absolute crazy stuff. I didn't get into that madness. Alison I was young and vulnerable" Mrs. O'Connell turns her head towards the window as if someone were watching her. "But there were others, much darker ones; they were filled with pure evil. They committed murders and tried to open a gate to Hades." Alison has now joined her mother in crying. "Alison you are all I have left in this world, please don't hate me."

Mrs. O'Connell continues, "Doctor Henderson's first son was murdered and after that he became very unstable. He convinced me to join the Brotherhood of the Enlightened with him. I was young and stupid. They used his grief against him and told him that if he killed all those children as a sacrifice that they could bring his first son back through a gate with the other world. So one day he finally did it, he killed all those children at the Asylum, including your brother, his second son" Mrs. O'Connell's heart is now weighed down by absolute grief. "They told me that Jeremy's body was riddled with holes and destroyed. The police officer said he stuck a gun in your brother's mouth and blew his head apart." Alison weeps uncontrollably after hearing this remark in such gruesome detail. "I never got to see him again. I wanted to hold his broken body once more but I never got the chance. Even at the funeral, we had to have a closed casket."

At hearing all of this Alison is overcome with a blanket of numbness.

Mrs. O'Connell continues the dark story, "Jeremy was born with special needs, so we cared for him at the hospital. He was different from the other children; he was deformed with only one eye and a malformed jaw bone."

Alison replies, "How could you do this?"

"I don't know Alison it was like I was possessed; it's the biggest regret of my life." "I'm sorry Alison."

"All this time I thought my brother died of natural causes. You said it was natural causes mom." These truths are too hard and heavy for her to hear.

Alison never suspected such a bombshell would ever be dropped on her. "Just tell me one thing mom, did father ever know the truth?"

"Yes he knew everything and he forgave me. He saved me from this cult. He saved my soul from their trap. After that fateful day I left the Brotherhood for good. Please Alison, find it in your heart to do the same as your father, please forgive me. I thought that if I told you the truth that you would hate me forever"

"Doctor Henderson was destroyed by the evil that was inside him. Please Alison stay away from the Asylum there are secrets at that place that even I don't know." Mrs. O'Connell looks Alison in the eyes for the first time, "Please forgive me baby."

Alison reaches over giving her mother a much needed hug, "I love you too, I am so sorry any of this happened. This is all so crazy mom!"

"Promise me Alison you will stay away from there, "Doctor Henderson's evil spirit is trapped there along with all the souls of those poor tormented children I just know it Alison. Please promise me."

Suddenly, as if a light bulb goes off inside her head Alison quickly responds, "B.E., that's it. Alex Hoard, his tattoo said B.E."

Mrs. O'Connell is now completely confused, "What are you talking about Alison? Leave it alone, your brain is always searching for connections. Leave it alone."

"Mom, you don't understand Alex's tattoo stood for the Brotherhood of the Enlightened. He was in that cult at one point and then I think he decided to leave. He killed all of those doctors because they were in the cult as well. He didn't want them to sacrifice any more children. Maybe he can help me figure out what to do."

Alison transfixes her stare into her mother's eyes, "Mom I have been haunted by the spirit's of those children. They call me to do something, something that I don't understand. Maybe Alex Hoard is the key to saving their souls."

Mrs. O'Connell rises to her feet. "Please Alison; leave that place alone, it's not safe. We should move away from here far away."

Alison hugs her mother once more, "Mom I have to figure out how to help them. Jeremy's soul is trapped inside the old Asylum as well." If she could, Alison felt she had to free them somehow. She picks up the phone next to the bed; she knew she had one friend who could help her into the prison to see Alex Hoard; it was John, he was always there for her when she needed him most, that time was now. The road ahead was now clearing a little but what it revealed to her mind's eye was dark, disturbing and deadly.

# Eleven

The large burly man throws Allen back into his room, slamming the door behind him. The door clicks locked, "Stay in your room you little bastard." The guard slowly walks down the hall thudding his size 15 shoes all the way down the hall.

"Welcome back buddy." Allen peels himself from the floor to see Goob standing there, thankfully wearing clothes this time and sporting a big black eye.

"Goob those bastards got Star. They stuck her in some room and drugged her up. They're crazy Goob. We have to get the hell out of here soon!"

Goob scratches his Mohawk, "I got news for ya buddy; we're all crazy."

Goob approaches Allen, "Why do you think our parents sent us up here, I mean there's no shock treatment or anything but basically they see us as mental patients." Allen walks over to the door and pulls on the knob, but it's locked. "We're trapped in here like rats." Allen walks over to the window to see how far the drop is.

"Did you know that rats have sex ten times a day?"

"I'm serious Goob we gotta get out of here."

Goob reaches under his bed, "Look, I was saving this for a rainy day but now seems like as good a time as ever to use it." He places the long board on his bed and pulls the sheet cover from the object revealing a Ouija board. "I'm going to attempt to communicate with my spirit guide Tobey." Allen gives Goob an extremely confused look. "You see Allen, he can tell us what's going on with Star; he's not restricted to a physical form so he can travel through time and space. He can go check on her and be back in no time and the best part is that no one will even know." Allen's look of confusion has now changed into interest. Allen places his hand on the communicator, joining Goob. "Tobey can you hear me, it's me Francis."

Allen laughs, "Francis, no wonder you go by Goob." "Shut up, we must be serious now." Goob's face turns completely red.

"Tell anyone my real name and I will kill you!" The piece slowly moves to the word "YES".

"Hello Tobey, we need to ask you a favor, can you help us?" The piece again moves to"YES".

Allen shakes his head in disbelief, "This is crazy Goob; you have to be moving it. It can't just move on its own. I don't belief in the spirit world."

"Shh, be quiet." Allen takes a big gulp.

"Tobey, there is a girl that we need you to find for us; she's trapped in the clinic. Can you go to her and tell us how she is?" The piece, twice as quickly as normal, moves over the word "NO."

"What does he mean? Goob ask him why not." Allen now a firm believer of the spirit world repeats himself, "Ask again Goob!"

Goob shakes his head, "Tobey why can't you go to her?" The piece moves around the board and spells out the word, "M-O-N-S-T-E-R."

"What does that mean? Is he talking about Dracula or something? Goob ask him to explain. What monster?"

Goob once again asks Tobey to explain himself, "Tobey what monster?"

Pillars of steam begin to rise from the surface of the board, the boys let go of the communicator as it slowly starts to crawl around the board on its' own spelling the word S-A-C-R-I-F-I-C-E. The boys could not believe what they were seeing; the piece jumping back and forth almost too fast to keep up with.

"Goob did you see that?" Then a second word came that was even more chilling than the first word, it was L-E-A-V-E. Goob was still shaking in disbelief.

"What do you think it all meant Goob?" Allen grabs Goob by the shoulders and commences to shake him out of his catatonic state. "I don't understand, what the hell is going on?" Allen runs to the door gripping and pulling the handle, trying to open the door. Goob quickly joins him. What could they do, they were trapped under house arrest and Star was trapped in her drug-induced sleep halfway across the courtyard. Their situation seemed hopeless.

John pulls to a screeching halt as he reaches Ally's apartment.

"Mom, he's here and I have to go."

Mrs. O'Connell grabs her arm pulling her back, "Alison, I can't stop you from going but—" The doorbell rings, "But I can go with you. I knew the man Alex Hoard when he was a boy. He lived with your brother at the hospital during the tragedy. He was one of the few to survive. As a man he was brainwashed into the Brotherhood even though as a child he was almost murdered by the same group." Mrs. O'Connell squeezes Alison's hand, "I have to go with you Alison!"

Alison smiles, "Are you sure mom? It may be dangerous."

"Yes dear, I am ready to face this." The two clasp hands, as if forming a new solidarity, they then quickly exit the apartment. As they head towards the prison, only hours before the execution of Alex Hoard, John questions Alison on what she expects to learn from this killer. He seems clueless to why they are trying to reach him.

"I just don't get it Ally, what are we looking for?" "John, the murderer at the Old Valley Asylum was a member of a group called the Enlightened Brotherhood. A weird look covers John's face when she mentions this. He glances to Mrs. O'Connell and then faces Alison once more.

"Alex Hoard has a tattoo that reads B.E. I don't think that that's a coincidence. Alex was also at the Asylum as a child."

John smiles, "Wow Ally, still the best investigator in the state."

A voice on the radio begins to talk about the Alex Hoard execution; "Tonight mass murderer Alex Hoard will face the electric chair for his killings spree which lasted two weeks claiming the life of over thirty doctors in four states."

Mrs. O'Connell puts her hand on Alison's shoulder, "Sweetheart, are you sure about doing this? Maybe we should turn around."

Alison replies in a comforting voice, "Yes mom, I am sure about doing this."

John floors the mini-van passing a state trooper hiding behind a billboard. The blaring of the officer's squad car is heard from behind the weary travelers.

"Oh shit, we got a Smokey on our tail. I guess it's time for my secret weapon."

Alison peers out the back of the van, "What's your secret weapon John?"

"Nitrous; hold on!" John opens a compartment revealing a blue switch, "Here we go!" He places his finger on the trigger sending 200 horsepower instantly to his four squealing tires, shooting the van down the freeway and far ahead of the police officer.

Mrs. O'Connell catches her breath, "Now what John?"

"Hold on." John pulls hard on the steering wheel sending the three off of the freeway and down the side embankment. The large grassy hill increases their speed to the point where John loses complete control. He slams on the brakes sending the van into a giant doughnut spiral, spitting grass everywhere. Despite all of this, somehow John is able to control the spin and keep the van from flipping completely over, they come to a jarring stop mere inches from the river below. A sigh of relief shared by all.

John unclenches his white knuckles from the steering wheel and opens his eyes, "Is everyone alright?"

Alison answers, "Just great Andretti!"

Her mother also replies, "I think I am still alive?"

John looks back up the hill, "It looks like we lost him, and only a fool would have tried something like that." Alison and Mrs. O'Connell give John the evil eye. "I mean, that was pretty brave, don't you think ladies?" John smirks after saying this.

The three slowly make it back to the freeway after miles of driving off-road and continue towards Alex Hoard hoping to make it there in time. After about an hour the prison comes into view. It is beckoning them to come closer.

"There it is John." Alison points at the prison as the large structure appears to them over the horizon. "That's where we'll find Alex." Alison's mother is now fast asleep; meanwhile John is rolling up a doobie getting ready to smoke up.

"So Ally what happened between you and your mom, you guys seem to be having some friction or something." John looks back to offer her a puff but she declines.

Alison looks at her mother and smiles, "Oh nothing John, I love her very much. We all make mistakes and I am trying to fix it." Alison shakes her head as if coming out of a daze and sighs loudly. "John we need to find out as much as we can learn about this Enlightened Brotherhood. I think they are the key to this."

John drops his doobie in his lap almost burning a hole in his pants. He quickly recovers the joint then responds.

"Ally do you think that this Alex guy is gonna tell you anything? I mean is messing with this Brotherhood really such a good idea? Maybe you should leave it alone."

"SCREECH." John slams on his brakes as a dark figure runs across the road nearly being squashed by the van.

"Holy Shit; who was that?"

Alison sticks her head out of the window, "John that was him?"

"Him who?"

Alison pulls her head back into the window, "Alex Hoard! Somehow he escaped! Follow him!"

Mrs. O'Connell slowly stretches, "What's going on? Did we hit something?"

"Mom, Alex Hoard just ran in front of us and we nearly ran him over!"

John still breathing heavy, "Ally should I follow him? I mean what if he has a weapon or something." Alison looks into the darkness surrounding them outside.

"I have to talk to him again!"

John throws the van in a half doughnut and smashes the acceleration as he jumps the curb and onto the field. They follow faster and faster until the outline of a very tall man can be seen in the light of the full moon entering into a cornfield directly ahead. Alex turns his head in the direction of the oncoming van and smiles; suddenly he springs into the corn and disappears. John slams on the brakes almost crushing the farmers barking wiener dog which has decided to block their path.

"Ally I don't think we should try to follow him anymore. Besides the cops will be swarming all over this place in no time!" Alison throws open the door and runs full speed into the corn, she quickly disappears into the large stalks ahead. John sits there in shock not knowing what to do at this point. He looks at Mrs. O'Connell dazed and confused.

As Alison runs through the corn she screams out for the fleeing man.

"Alex Hoard please don't run I need to talk to you, please don't run."

She can hear the sound of breaking corn stalks all around her; she struggles to move forward even as her fear has begun to take over her adrenaline. John reaches into his glove compartment and pulls out an old revolver. The crackling of thunder can be heard approaching the field of corn. Another rain storm is fast on their heels.

"Mrs. O'Connell stay here and lock the doors, I'm going after Ally." Johns jumps from the van keeping his gun in plain view for all to see. Mrs. O'Connell locks the doors and begins to frantically roll up the windows. John enters the cornfield sweat burning his eyes and fear filling his stomach. Alison continues to yell out for Alex, without warning she stumbles into a large grass area void of any corn stalks. In the middle of the field Alison sees a large barn and what appears to be a man heading inside. She takes a deep breath and heads toward the barn. As Alison enters the old structure she can hear the sounds of mice scurrying around the large stacks of hay. The wind howling in her ears as if it were the voice of a thousand souls. In the rafters above the sound of an owl coming bellowing down falls upon the frightened woman.

In the blink of an eye a hairy hand covers Alison's mouth and she is sent flying into a pile of manure. The man turns Alison around to face him; it was Alex Hoard he was bleeding profusely from his side. Alex had been shot during his successful attempt to escape the prison. Alison scared stiff at this point could not even conjure an intelligible sentence. The wounded man looks around the barn searching for something.

"You have to find, the book."

Alison is now able to eek out a few words. "What book?"

Alex coughs up some blood and attempts to finish his thought. "It will help destroy the…" Alison grabs him by the shoulders as he seems to slide into a coma.

"Destroy the what?" Alex finds the strength to continue turning bluer every second. He tries to rise to his feet but falls to the ground.

"The evil that lies buried at the Asylum. The Brotherhood will attempt to appease their Demons with the sacrifice of the children and drinking the blood of their innocence out of a skull." Alex begins to cough again, each time with increasing intensity. "The time is near, once enough innocent blood is spilled, the gateway to the other world will be opened. You must find and destroy the high priest and speak the sacred words at the gate before it can be opened. I have tried my whole life to destroy the men in the Brotherhood but I never found the High Priest; he has hidden himself where I could never find him. I once worshipped at their dark masses with so many others and now I die trying to destroy them."

Alison replies, "I will stop them, I promise Alex, she cradles the dying behemoth on her lap, "I am not alone. They killed my brother Jeremy as a child during the Asylum Massacre."

A single tear falls from his mangled face as he realizes who Alison is. "I was once called Jeremy as a boy. I was kept at the Valley Asylum away from the world. I was just a dirty secret. When I left the Asylum, they lied and said that I had died but I survived that dreaded day. I have thought about that day my entire life, I remember a tall man placing a gun into my mouth and then he looked deeply into my eyes, he fell on the floor and then died, he was my own father. I was taken from the Asylum and raised into the Brotherhood where I was trained to kill for their blood thirsty causes, but one day I woke up and turned on them. I was brainwashed my whole life." Alison never knowing her brother felt like she had died on the inside; hearing that this man was her long lost sibling made her cry, but they were tears of not only immense sadness but also joy.

"Oh Jeremy I always longed to find you. This is all such a nightmare!" She squeezes him closer as he begins to slip away. "Mother and I love you so much; she thought that you died long ago." "No she didn't. They took our innocence and they will try to take all the innocence from this world and replace it with death. I only wish I had another chance at life. To live again as someone else."

Alison feels a strong tug on her hair. From behind she's lifted to her feet and then thrown down on the dirt once more.

"Oh Ally, you had to dig and dig didn't you?" Alison is shocked to see John standing there with gun in hand. He turns his attention from Alison to aim the pistol at the fallen Jeremy Henderson. "And you, did you really think that you could stop us? We are everywhere! You had to tell Alison everything so now I have to kill her too, I actually liked her."

"THUMP" John falls to the ground; the shovel that Alison has used to knock him out with has left a nice dent in the side of his skull.

Alison runs over to Jeremy, "Where is this book?"

He points to the upper level of the barn, "Climb up the ladder, it should be hidden in a wooden chest. You must hurry the police will be here soon, I left a trail of blood."

Alison squeezes his hand, "I will finish this brother, I promise." She kisses him on the forehead and heads to the ladder; she begins to climb the frail structure. The old ladder shakes and sways as she reaches the top. She scans the area until she spots a wooden chest. "That's got to be it." Alison runs over and opens the old container; inside she sees an old book with strange symbols on the cover. Alison retrieves the book and in doing so she reveals a surprisingly shinny dagger hiding underneath it. Alison takes the two objects and slowly heads down the ladder. She reaches the ground and to her horror the body of her one time friend Jonathan is nowhere to be found, Jeremy lie there however, his body lifeless and pale.

She looks to her fallen brother, "I promise to make it right Jeremy. I will return for you." Alison makes her way towards the barn exit, trying to be as silent as possible. She reaches the doors looks in both directions and begins to run for the van hoping that her mother was still there.

"Hey Ally!" A booming voice is heard coming from behind her. Alison stops dead in her tracks then turns around as John exits the cornfield and aims his weapon straight at her forehead. "Alison, Alison, I want to tell you how sorry I am that this had to end this way, I always wanted to sleep with you but I guess I'll never get my chance."

Alison still in shock by her friend's betrayal, "You bastard John, how could you?"

"It was really a no brainer, I mean I was supposed to keep an eye on you and if you found out too much, well then I was supposed to take care of it!" John walks closer to Alison, gun still pointing at her head. "That night that you got hit by lightning, well it wasn't a lightning bolt. It was a Pete Rose edition bat.

Everyone is in on this thing, even the doctors that cared for your "lightning strike coma". We are at the dawn of a new age Alison, an age based on power and blood. Your own mother is a big part of this thing. She's been keeping an eye on you for all these years protecting you from the truth. You see Ally your blood will be spilled for the cause, and drunk from the crystal skull. You are a pure blood, a blue blood lineage."

Alison is blown away by this revelation but very suspicious, "I don't believe you John; my mother left the cult a long time ago?" John places his revolver on her wet skin. Alison grits her teeth then closes her eyes, "John, you bastard, I thought we were friends!" Alison closes her eyes in total disbelief at what he has told her.

"It was all for the cause Ally. Goodbye sweetie!" He clicks back the trigger. "Into the great unknown you go. I'll try not to spill too much; we will need the rest for later."

Like a freight train hitting a small deer the body of Jonathan is broken and smashed as the van plows into his side and over his frame, crushing him instantly. Alison is also sent flying as the impact of the collision forces her into the cornfield. Mrs. O'Connell leaps from the driver's seat and rushes to aid her fallen daughter.

"Alison are you alright baby?"

Alison hugs her mother trying to control her tears, "Mom I'm ok, John, he, he, he was in the Brotherhood. He said that you were still with them. He would have killed me if you didn't…" Alison, with the help of her mother hobbles back into the van, "Mother, I just saw Jeremy."

Samantha O'Connell (aka Mrs. O'Connell) is shocked by this statement, "What do you mean Alison? That's absurd; he died a long time ago!" Alison grabs her mother's shoulders and looks her dead in her face.

"I mean that Alex Hoard is actually Jeremy. They lied to you when they told you that he was killed, he survived. Mrs. O'Connell is shocked by this statement. The shock then mutates into disappointment and then into laughter; with the cackle of a witch she responds. Her entire expression now completely transformed.

"You are so smart aren't you Alison! You are just like your real father, always snooping around." Alison squeaks out the words, "What did you say?"

"What are you talking about mother?"

Mrs. O'Connell shakes her head her leathery features seem to pulsate in the moonlight like a reptile, "John didn't lie to you when he told you that I was still in the Brotherhood, in fact I am the high priest or should I say priestess. I have many servants like your friend John. She pushes Alison down into the back seat of the van and hovers over her like a vulture circling its prey.

"I have been grooming you since birth so that you could be the key and open the gate. I had to keep you ignorant of the truth because the sacrifice requires innocent blood to fill the skull. Innocent or ignorant it's all the same. I seduced Dr. Henderson to kill all those children to appease the Dark one and soon I will sacrifice you to open the gate to Hades. He will rule this dimension and I will be his queen." Alison's face is covered in complete horror.

"Now that you know Alison it is time to fulfill your destiny. Don't fight it!" Mrs. O'Connell looks towards the barn; the final resting place of her son Jeremy. "The worst part is that I wish you never would have discovered the truth about your brother. I blame John for that, he should never have given you the assignment to cover the story of Alex Hoard the mass murderer, that's why I killed him, he has always been sloppy, leading you into the Asylum that night, I should have killed him then. I was watching you that night, you heard me howling in the trees. Mommy can take many forms Alison. When you entered the Asylum you stirred the spirits of the children much too soon." The face of Samantha O'Connell begins to change into that of a much younger woman. She grabs Alison by the throat squeezing her tightly, "And then tonight he almost spilled your blood using a pistol. The sacrifice requires magical words and a knife and I see you brought them both to me." Alison realizes that her mother has taken both of those sacred objects from her. She had lost them in the collision when she was sent flying to the ground.

"And if you were wondering I am really your mother, I just never loved you. I hated faking it all these years. You are a pawn my dear and I am the Queen."

Alison bellows out a cry for help, "Scream all you want no one will save you!" Beneath the van an arm reaches out pulling Mrs. O'Connell to the wet grass below. Her face smashes to the earth with a thunderous crash. Alison quickly hops out of the van.

It is Jeremy her loving brother, he yells to her, "Go Alison save them!" Jeremy holds on to Mrs. O'Connell's body trying to give Alison time to escape. Alison jumps into the front seat of the still running van.

"Thank you Jeremy." The siblings exchange a loving look and then Alison throws the van into reverse and backs speedily towards the main road. Alison was lucky to grab the book which she almost forgot in all the madness of the last few moments. The fingernails of Mrs. O'Connell begin to stretch to inhuman lengths as well as her teeth. She is transforming right before Jeremy into a creature from another world. The monster easily subdues the man turns its aggression on him.

"My dear son you should have stayed in your place!" She crushes Jeremy's throat with her powerful fangs killing him instantly. Alison however has managed to escape the devilish woman, for now.

Just as quickly as Mrs. O'Connell had transformed into the hideous beast she has returned to her normal frail appearance. She spits out a mouthful of Jeremy's blood and slowly walks toward the road.

"No matter where you go, I will find you Alison." A black limo seems to materialize out of the night air and the woman enters the back door and then disappears in a flash of light. The race to save the children has begun but can Alison stop her destiny or will it control her and swallow her whole?

# Twelve

The weary woman finally reaches her apartment complex where she ditches John's van in the back parking lot; she continues on foot until she reaches her car. From this point on she knew that she couldn't trust anyone. In one day everything had changed, all the killing and horrific revelations had begun to harden her heart, but she would not give up. She had to save the world from the Brotherhood and she had to stop her mother somehow. The woman she thought had loved her all those years was really using her for her own sick twisted reasons; Alison was to be sacrificed to some evil God.

Alison reaches into her pocket and pulls out the keys to her baby. She enters the Mustang and turns the ignition. The growl of the V-8 seems to bring to life a sleeping beast. She fixes her rearview as she turns the corner leaving her complex. All she can think of is the face of her brother. He wasn't as bad as the world thought him to be. In fact he tried to save the world and by his own sacrifice he had redeemed himself, in her eyes at least. The Brotherhood had used him as a pawn in their sick ritual killings. Jeremy was just the tool they used.

"Dame es contas eskenus lom antes" Alison tried to memorize the ancient text from the sacred book. These words had to be spoken before the knife was driven into the heart of the high priestess. The fact that she had to kill her mother was just beyond her comprehension. She wasn't sure if this could even be done. She had never been a violent person but she knew that she had to do this to save the lives of the living and to release the souls of the deceased. The biggest problem that she was facing was that she didn't even have possession of the knife she had to retrieve it somehow.

This dark cult had to be stopped before the gateway to their demon world could be opened. As Alison pulled to the next light she noticed a dark sedan following closely behind. She had no idea if it was anything to worry about but the way it was following her made her suspicious. She slowly pressed on the gas accelerating to about 55; the dark car simultaneously increased his speed as well.

Alison checked her rearview just as she felt a jolt forcing her face into the steering wheel. She blacked out momentarily but regained consciousness immediately.

The pursing sedan smashes into her rear bumper nearly causing Alison to lose control of the vehicle. She tightens her grip on the wheel gaining back her control of the road, blood now dripping from her forehead Alison smashes the gas pedal causing smoke to escape from her rear wheel well. The mustang surges ahead leaving a small gap between her and the sedan. Up ahead the light that was green only seconds ago turns yellow then quickly red. She knows that there is no way she's going to stop and let her pursuers trap her in the traffic ahead. Alison closes her eyes and presses the gas pedal to its' extreme limit.

"Oh God please help me!"

"HONK, HONK."

Two trucks swerve around Alison narrowly colliding with her mustang. The black sedan slams on its brakes, but to no avail the sliding car slams into the back of a pickup truck sending the sedan flipping end over end finally landing on its roof in a nearby ditch and then exploding into a huge fireball. Alison opens her eyes to great relief; she heard the honking of the truck but only saw the back of her eyelids as she narrowly escaped a fiery death. For the moment she felt like James Bond but then the dark reality crept back in to her fragile brain. She was most likely heading to her own death. This was hard to swallow. A few months ago she was a successful reporter and writer; at least she had some new material for her next book. She hoped she'd be alive to write it!

The voice on the radio that seconds earlier was that of a cheesy and over excited Viagra taking DJ transformed into that of a small child, "It will open soon." It was like the station or frequency had changed for a split second and that is what happened, the souls of the children trapped in that evil place were reaching for a release before they were trapped forever by the opening of the gate to Hades.

"Help me God!"

Alison remembered being inside the Asylum that stormy night when a candle appeared and saved her from the tiny demon. She remembered the children in all of her nightmares and now she knew that all this time that they had been trying to communicate with her so that she could release them and also stop the Demons from entering our world. What a fate for those poor souls, trapped forever in the depravity of an evil mind.

She takes a deep breath, "Please protect me Jeremy!" Alison takes a right and enters the freeway, the freeway that led directly to the Asylum, the freeway that led to her destiny. In less than an hour she would arrive at the old Asylum and then all Hell would break loose, unless she stopped it!

"Enter." A tall man wearing a dark robe enters the private quarters of Tyler Hoffman.

"My Lord, she is here! She says that the time is near for us to unleash the great one onto this world for its ultimate judgment." Tyler turns his leather chair to face his loyal servant.

"Yes you fool soon we will open the gate, but remember the power we unleash can only be controlled by me, the High Priest, The Demon will enter into my body and not hers, so I suggest you remain on my good side if you know what's good for you."

"But my Lord she is the Priestess the bride of the Beast."

Tyler stands to his feet, "Silence you insolent fool, the Beast will be inside me, therefore I am the Beast and she and all else will be submissive to me!" Tyler walks over to the window slowly raising the blinds. "Look at those children out there; they have no idea what horror awaits them. Their innocent blood will make a complete sacrifice. We will raise the demons with our summoning powers tonight and they in turn will sacrifice the children for us."

The man wearing black smiles and responds, "And once they are satisfied we will be given the key to the gate and then…"

Tyler turns to the man grabbing him by the throat, "And then you fool I will open the gate unleashing the beast, and I alone will be the man who controls the power of the universe not the Priestess." Tyler releases his grip, "I stand alone."

The servant drops to his knees, "Yes my Lord, you alone can control the Beast of ages."

Tyler opens his closet to reveal a crimson robe, "Now leave me, I have much planning to do for tonight's ceremony. Make sure no one escapes there must be a complete fulfillment or else we will not receive the key."

The robed man stands to his feet, "Do not worry once the spirits are released no child will escape I will electrify the perimeter gate."

Tyler grins with sadistic pleasure, "Good now leave me. I must prepare."

The man leaves just before the double doors of Tyler's office swing open furiously, a woman wearing a silky crimson dress enters the room and with each step she transforms from the old shape of Mrs. O'Connell to a voluptuous and seductive Samantha, the High Priestess of the Brotherhood of the Enlightened.

"From an old woman to the most beautiful woman of all time, how do you do it?" Tyler bows before her. "Your Highness everything is going as planned."

Tyler bows once more, "Soon we will let loose the hounds of hell to prey upon the children and once they have had their fill then we will sacrifice Alison. And then…"

Samantha interrupts him rudely, "And then my servant, our dark Lord will enter into your body and we shall rule the universe for eternity. But remember you are but a vessel a body to hold the true ruler."

Tyler hides a scowl under his lips, "I presume that Alison is already here then."

"Tyler you presume too much I think." She burns him with her glare as if she were reading his thoughts of greed and supreme power.

Tyler looks to the floor, "I only aim to serve you High Priestess."

She places her hands on his shoulders, "I hope so, for your sake." She slowly circles him sliding her hands down his back. "Don't worry she will be here soon. She won't be able to stay away. Her need to be a hero is sickening but at least it's predictable" Samantha walks to the window and watches the children playing outside.

Tyler responds quickly, "How do you know that she'll come here?"

Samantha, formerly Mrs. O'Connell smiles, "Because she is my daughter."

As Alison reaches the outskirts of the Asylum grounds she pulls her car over less then a mile from the front gate. The thick forest surround most of the gate perimeter, Alison knows she must sneak in away from the main openings to have any hope of entering undetected. She pulls a map out of her glove box revealing a network of sewer tunnels, two of them leading straight into the old Asylum basement. She hoped it still led there; right now all she had was faith and hope and she needed both to continue on.

Alison looks heavenward, "God I know that I've never really prayed to you before but if you can hear me then please help me, I need you now more then ever. Please guide me." Alison closed her eyes and took a deep breath.

She leaves the car and slides into the forest heading towards the sewer entrance. The sound of foraging animals and tree top birds fills the air. Alison drops to the ground at hearing a different sound, the sound of footsteps. She manages to crawl under some nearby bushes avoiding detection.

"Make sure you check the entire area." Alison spots two men wearing black military uniforms combing the forest looking for something or someone. She didn't want to be around to see what or who it was they were seeking. At her first opportunity Alison makes a b-line for the sewer entrance, sweating profusely all the way.

The entrance was a giant concrete circle; flowing brown water fell out of the pipe and cascaded ten feet below into another sewer opening. She would have to take a running jump if she were going to make it inside the pipe, which hung over the cavernous drop off. Alison tightens her shoelaces and takes a deep breath.

"I hope one year on the track team pays off." She does the sign of the cross and springs to her feet. Alison starts her run pushing her body to its very limits. She reaches her top speed just as she catapults herself into the air. Her arms stretch as she reaches out for the sewer pipe. Her frame begins to drop as gravity takes control of her flying body. The pipe, which was once foot level, now becomes eye level. Alison realizes that her attempt was coming up a few inches too short. With one last gasp to salvage her jump she nearly hyper extends her arms as she somehow manages to grip the very bottom of the pipe.

Alison swings underneath the pipe, still holding on for dear life, she smashes chest first into the underbelly of this concrete entrance way. The brown water flows freely on top of her head. The stench of human waste fills her nostrils; Alison has to fight with all her strength to keep her lunch where it is. Her brittle fingers slowly give way one at a time. She is about to fall crashing down to the pipes below. She is too tired to hold on. Is this how her journey would end, covered in shit and falling to her death?

Without warning two arms reach down from inside the pipe and slowly pull Alison inside. The jagged bottom of the pipe slices and tears at Alison's legs as she enters the tunnel. Blood from her wounds turn the brown waterfall red as it cascades over the side. To her astonishment a young man stands before her huffing and puffing after his hero like rescue of her. She graciously thanks the boy, happy to still be alive.

"Who are you?"

"I'm Allen; I was trapped inside that so called summer camp so I'm trying to escape and bring some help back."

Alison responds immediately, "So where does this tunnel come out?"

Allen turns his head towards the tunnel, "Into a basement. I was trapped in my room and my roommate and I started a fire with a lighter, when they unlocked the door to put it out we escaped. I hid in the basement where I found an old drain. I managed to open it and close it behind me."

Alison shakes her head, "Where's your roommate?"

Allen's face changes from exhaustion to fear, "I don't know, I heard screams and then nothing. I just kept running. I wanted to escape so I could find help.

I should have helped him but I was so terrified that my adrenaline took over and I ran away."

Alison grabs Allen by the shoulders, "Allen there is no time to find help. They are going to kill all of those children."

Allen pulls back from her grip, "What do you mean kill them all?"

Alison replies, "They are in a cult, they think by sacrificing all the kids that their spirit demons will give them the key to open a gate to hell. It's a really long story!"

Allen begins to cry, "Oh no, Star!"

"Who's Star?"

Allen turns to Alison looking her directly in the eyes, "A girl I love." Allen looks at Alison, "As crazy as your story sounds I believe it for some reason, I had a nightmare just like what you described the night right before I came to this evil place but I thought it was caused from those Pot brownies that I had."

With this knowledge now in his possession Allen turns toward the darkness, "Come on we have to save them."

The sound of men speaking begins to circulate inside the pipe, Alison knows the men outside are closing in on them, and so she hurriedly follows behind her young rescuer into the unknown. The darkness now surrounded them completely.

The long pipe seems to go on for days she thought to herself as the two made their way towards a faint light up ahead. The drain opening allowed a small amount of light to enter. As they reached the opening Allen peered around the room to make sure that no one was inside. As he pushes the drain upward a deep growl begins to echo from inside the tunnel, the very tunnel that they are standing in. Alison focuses her attention in the direction of the eerie noise. The sounds become louder and louder as the splash of water can also be heard as if something with a great stride neared closer.

"Hurry Allen! Something is down here!"

The boy struggles with the drain, "I think it's stuck."

Two glowing ovals appear now, set apart like the eyes of a panther.

"Shit!" Alison grabs the drain, "Ok, one, two, go!" The two push the drain sending the cover flying into the room. Allen followed by Alison quickly escape; leaping from the floor opening and into the basement above. The two quickly grab the previously discarded drain cover placing it atop the gaping hole. As soon as Allen completes this task a dark beast lunges for his hands nearly biting his fingers completely off. Allen falls back as the creature smashes its face into the steel drain cover almost knocking it free. The flickering light bulb above sways back and forth as if being tossed from first to second base.

"What the hell was that?"

Alison answers, "It wasn't snoopy?" The drain cover is now placed snuggly blocking the creature from entering the basement, at least for now. The two climb the stairs cautiously out of the basement and reach the first floor. Alison touches Allen on the shoulder trying to get his attention.

"Look Allen, go find Star and get out of here, I have to find Tyler Hoffman and my mother and end this ritual before it's too late."

"You mean the big greasy guy who runs this place?"

Alison shakes her head, "Yes that asshole!"

Allen points to the door at the end of the hall, "Take that exit and head for the main tower, he's probably up in his ivory tower." Allen extends his hand to Alison, "Good luck, I'll try to get the kids out, you take care of that bastard."

Alison smiles, "Good luck Allen." With the hallway clear Alison heads towards the exit as Allen runs in the opposite direction. She reaches the door slowly turning the knob, the door swings open, "All clear she thinks to herself." Alison takes one step outside when without warning her head is greeted by a shattering blow. Everything once again fades out of focus. She drops to the ground completely unconscious. The wet floor greets her face with a resounding THUD. Alison once again has lost total control of the situation.

When Alison regains her facilities she is surrounded by total darkness. She touches her head feeling the ooze of her own blood. She needs to start wearing a helmet she thinks to herself. It feels like she is inside a prison holding cell only stinkier.

Alison feels her way around the room until she touches what seems to be a crack under some sort of door, "Help me, can anyone hear me?" Only the sound of her own voice echoes back to her. She hopes that Allen had better luck then her and had hoped he had at least escaped with his love Star. Alison was trapped like a rat and now she was without the book and the knife.

# Thirteen

The campers, unaware of the danger that was present all around them, poured into the swimming pool. It was the first day that they were allowed to swim. The limit stated twenty kids at a time but there where more like forty of them all crammed and splashing in the blue water. A lone lifeguard sat there in the chair. He could hardly stay awake; he was dozing in and out of his afternoon siesta. And as he was having one of his five-minute power naps a few of the campers were able to sneak out of the pool area.

The lifeguard was only awakened when one of the campers splashed him with a giant cannonball. The screaming and yelling was deafening, arms and legs flailed around sending a torrent of pool water into the air like rain. The lifeguard slowly closed his eyes entering into another sleep mode. Just as he fell back into slumber, the swimmers; as if being pulled under the water by a giant octopus, in an instant, are sucked into the depths and disappear without a trace into a black hole. The silence becomes deafening. The lifeguard sitting in his chair snoring away never noticing a thing until another large splash covers his body drenching him from head to toe.

He jumps up fully awakened by the giant splash noticing his shirt has changed from white to red; a crimson pool lay beneath him where a crystal clear swimming pool once was. He looks into the water looking for any signs of life but notices nothing until the center of the red water begins to circulate forming a giant whirlpool. The force from the vortex begins to suck towels and shoes into the center strengthening to the point where the frightened man begins to feel a tug on his shorts pulling him towards the pool.

He grabs the side of his chair holding on with all his might. His legs have begun to dangle in the air, the whirlpool suction has reached hurricane force, the man cannot fight the pull any longer; he's sucked into the water right as Allen appears outside the pool gate area just barely missing this terrible sight, in fact he saw nothing. The whirlpool ceases its suction ending its rotation. Allen leaps the fence to see the red water before him but oblivious of what he narrowly missed.

"What the fuck is that?" Near the side of the pool a white arm shoots out of the water. Allen dives to the lone survivor grabbing the extended hand and pulling outward. Allen falls backwards revealing the arm, unattached to any body. He releases his grip from the white appendage and quickly leaps to his feet and books it back onto the surrounding fence; falling over the other side and landing on his back. With the wind knocked out of him Allen rests there gasping for his breath. He had never seen such a horrible sight in his life. It made him think about Star even more, would he ever see her again? His heart was heavy but he knew he couldn't let his fear hold him back.

He stands to his feet using the fence to pull himself upright. Allen looks upwards towards the dormitories; lights from various rooms seem to be pulsating off and on, off and on, Allen hears screams from various rooms as well, "Oh my God it's all begun."

Bubba (AKA Max) the biggest bully in camp, sits on his bed eating his lunch, "I hate swimming and I'm glad I could cut out today, I was starving. Those dummies are probably swimming laps or something pointless like that right now. Losers!"

As bubba reaches into his bag of chips he feels something sticky. It felt like earthworms, the very kind of earthworms that he would put down kids pants when he was back in school. Completely disgusted by this, Bubba throws his brown bag on the floor.

"What the hizell was that?" The boy watches in horror as the bag begins to move across the floor completely by itself. He pulls his dangling feet onto the bed and presses his back against the wall. Bubba was about to pee his pants big time.

"What the?" The bag has begun to pulsate like a human heart, it starts to shake as if it was a volcano preparing to explode, and then it just stops. Bubba peers over the side of the bed at the lunch sack, his own heart ready to explode. He stretches his pudgy hands out to grab the bag; his trembling fingers pull the bag from the floor and he places it on top of his bed. Bubba gently pulls the sack open and looks inside. Staring back at him is what appears to be the face of a man with red glowing eyes, Bubba screams in terror at this horrific sight. This wasn't what his mom had packed. Bubba began to piss his pants.

The bag bursts into flames charring the poor boys fingers; a large pile of ash now covers his bed sheets. Bubba out of instinct and fear jumps out of the bed and makes a mad dash for his door, his chest of drawers slide in front of the exit to block his escape. The furniture was now moving on its own, possessed by an unseen hand. Bubba grabs them with his wounded hands and tries to push them aside but this unseen force holds them in place. He screams out in pain and horror. The full-length mirror in the corner of his room begins to emanate a dark red light shooting out in all directions covering Bubba's frightened face with a crimson mask of color and fear Bubba turns to the mirror panting heavily as the reflection of a creature appears to him. He has become paralyzed as this evil demon stares him in his tear filled eyes. Bubba trembles with ferocious fear.

This creature looks like a half man half panther monster, it snarls at him revealing it's long yellow fangs as it methodically steps through the mirror and into Bubba's reality. The poor boy at that moment releases a steady stream of urine down his leg. His adrenaline flow also hits an all time high at the sight of such horror.

Bubba places his hands back onto the drawers and with all the might that he can muster he throws his shoulder into the wooden obstacle like his old football coach taught him during practice and drives them out of his way. The adrenaline that Bubba has built up inside his 300 lb frame explodes as he not only crumbles the drawers but bursts through the wooden door knocking it completely off of the frame and sending it flying into the hallway.

"Can you guys keep it down; I'm trying to become one with the universe?" The creature turns around to see Bubba's roommate walk out of the bathroom obviously stoned with joint in hand. "Wow this is some crazy Jamaican shit?"

The beast lashes out at the white Rasta man and with the flick of his wrist splits him in half sending each half flying into opposite corners of the room. Seeing his chance to flee Bubba has begun to labor down the hall, sweat pouring down his face, stinging his bloodshot eyes. A loud growl is released from the creature; the shockwaves burst one of Bubba's eardrums. Bubba screams out in a painful cry for help. All he can do is run.

The trembling boy finally reaches the back courtyard exit and leaves the building, the sounds of the pursuing beast on his heels. He looks around frantically for someone, anyone, to help him. In this state of fear and delusion he finds no one. He surveys the thick forest behind the dormitory building and decides that the cover of the trees is his best chance for survival. Miraculously he finds his way into the woods dropping in a ditch behind a giant oak tree. The sound of the door swinging open and slamming into the wall fills his one good ear. The glass inside the doorframe shatters covering the walkway with jagged shards, the sound of the falling pieces makes Bubba think of a giant claw ripping and tearing into his chest. The voice of the howling creature soon follows; the frightened boy curls into the fetal position. Bubba places his hand over his mouth trying to muffle the sounds of his heavy breathing and crying. Bubba's thoughts run wild in his simple mind; his thoughts were telling him to get as far away from this place as possible. The only problem was that he was too afraid to move, his body was paralyzed with fear.

The eyes of the woman finally began to adjust to the dark room. As Alison tugged on her ropes she began to realize that it was getting her nowhere. The chair was bolted to the floor and the knots on her wrist could not be untied especially because they were tied behind her back. Alison scans the room looking for anything that she could use to get out of her chair. In the center of the room was an alter covered with a red satin sheet, adorning the walls of this castle like room were many weapons of the dark ages, swords and shields, one shield in particular caught her attention simply because the face of a man was painted on it. The face she knew too well, it was Tyler Hoffman's.

"Well, well, well, glad you could make it Alison." Alison trembles at the voice; she knew exactly who it was.

"You sick bitch, killing all these poor children."

Samantha, formerly her mom, walks in front of Alison and grabs her by the jaw, "My dear, is that how you talk to your own mother, besides you are a little behind, the killings have already commenced. I have been listening to the screams of those poor spirits for the last hour or so. The evil ones are ahead of schedule; they have taken their victims and have satisfied the first part of the blood sacrifice, you being the final part. You know it's too bad because tomorrow was supposed to be parents' night!" The woman reaches into her pocket and slowly pulls from it the sacred knife.

"A short time from now I will perform the right of passage and your blood will be drunk from the crystal skull. This will open the gate and allow my master to come through." Tyler begins to laugh a devilish laugh. The two women turn their attention to the new guest as he enters the room.

"And then the beast will come forth as king on earth."

Alison turns to her mother, "You won't be able to control it. This Evil is to powerful!" Alison squirms and attempts in vain to free herself from the chair.

Tyler opens his mouth to reveal a serpent shaped tongue; it begins to slide out of his wide orifice and towards her face. Alison quickly looks away from him as she feels the slimy thing lick her from chin to forehead. "Maybe there are things Alison that you don't know about me." He pulls his serpentine tongue from her face, "I will see you tonight, just sit tight, you will bare witness to the end of life as the world has ever known it and the beginning of a new age." Tyler and Samantha seemingly float out of the room slamming the door behind them. Alison tugs on her ropes trying desperately to break free. She knows that she must escape and kill Tyler and Samantha before they can complete the ceremony. Time was running out and hope was fading fast.

Alison begins to weep as she struggles to escape; the ropes burning her hands as she pulls with all her strength. It was no use, she couldn't get loose. Alison notices as blue colored smog begins to roll in from under the door of her cell room. It fills her nostrils causing her to cough and choke. From this smog the outline of a small boy appears, he becomes more apparent as the figure approaches the scared woman. Alison can tell that this is a small child and not a figment of her imagination. His face is distorted by the smog but he seems very young. The little boy touches the ropes binding her down causing them to fall away, releasing her instantly. She grabs her wrist, falling to the floor still trying to catch her breath. The boy reaches over touching Alison on her cheek instantly filling her face with a warm energy, which quickly spreads throughout her entire body. She looks for the first time at the face of this guardian angel.

The boy smiles and opens his small mouth, "Save them Alison, they need you now." The boy looks sadly towards the floor shuffling his feet, "Or we will be trapped here forever!" The young boy slowly begins to fade away.

Alison reaches out and touches the boy on his translucent arm, "Who are you?"

The sound of thunder can be heard from above the room, "I am…"

The door of the cell slams open to reveal a tall man wearing a dark cloak and carrying a long spear with a black tip. Alison turns to where the blue boy was standing but he has completely vanished now. On the ground where he was standing only moments ago lay a small glowing candle. Alison grabs the candle as the man in black rushes to stop her. The flame from the candle seems to shoot forth like an oil gusher from the wick and with a giant explosion it burns the arms of her approaching attacker; he in kind turns his sharp tip towards her stomach desperately trying to impale her on the spear. Alison ducks to the floor letting the guard's momentum carry him crashing into the red alter in the center of the room causing his spear to be loosened from his grip and sending him falling to the floor. Alison feels a rush of supernatural energy now enter her body.

She leaps for the spear confiscating the deadly weapon from the dark figure. The assailant responds by pulling an ancient sword from off of the wall and once more charges Alison with deadly intent. The man lets out his fiercest battle cry as he thunders towards her now. She closes her eyes, "Guide me spirit!" Alison releases the spear towards her oncoming attacker. By either chance or divine intervention the weight and force of the throw causes the spear to pass completely through the man's throat killing him instantly; the body of the dead man falls into Alison knocking her to the floor, its limbs flailing as if he were still alive. She scrambles to push the carcass off of her as she rises to her feet. The warmth from the mysterious child still seems to still flow through her entire body. An aura of energy begins to emanate from her skin and extends into the surrounding atmosphere. She is shocked at the physical transformation as she looks her body over. It made her feel a strange sense of peace and comfort though still trapped in this violent situation.

"What is happening to me?" Alison looks to her hands noticing a blue tint to her fingers, not to mention everything else on her body. She could feel the presence of the child as if he were inside her, a part of her.

Alison closes her eyes, "Don't worry child, I already know who you are."

In the corner of the room the child appears once more, he smiles at Alison raising his right arm and speaking, "A door can be opened." A blue dust devil forms out of the surrounding ground around Alison and begins to swirl around the child.

Alison screams out to him, "A door to where?" The intensity of the dust devil has increased enormously. Alison can hardly keep her eyes open, the wind intensity still increasing like a twister. She felt like Dorothy trapped in Oz and longed for her home; she thought about Mango and hoped he was ok. When death faces you it is strange of what one thinks about. She took a deep breath; and just listened and what she heard was the spirits final words, "Fate's door to open and change" With a puff of smoke the room becomes silent as the boy disappears completely. Alison falls to her knees and slumps her head down between her shoulders. She places her hands over her eyes and wipes away her tears. "I must open the door." The strong conviction of rectifying the evil that has been done forces Alison to her feet. She takes in the deepest breath of her life and moves forward. Slowly forward.

# Fourteen

As Allen reaches the main tower he's sees what looks like a fire works display coming from inside Tyler Hoffman's office windows; red and yellow lights illuminating the room. He looks around the court yard which is now as silent and as lifeless as a black hole. It seemed as if he may be too late to save anyone.

"I hope I'm not too late.

Allen takes a deep breath and enters the main tower. The interior of the building has taken on a dark gloomy appearance. The floors have turned midnight black and the walls that were once covered with wood are now red as dragon's blood and as Allen also finds out, wet to the touch. He climbs the many floors of stairs until he reaches the camp infirmary where he last saw his beloved Star. The lights of the room begin flickering on and off. Allen does his best to stay out of sight as he enters the room where Star was strapped to the bed. He cannot tell if she is still there however. A figure lay still underneath the covers but he can't tell who or what it is. Allen grabs a needle from atop a medical tray and approaches the bed cautiously. With a firm grip on the needle he reaches out with his free hand and grabs the corner of the blanket, pulling it quickly to the floor. The needle falls out of his grip as Allen crashes to his knees.

Allen's stream of tears begin to fill the room, "Why, Why her?" Before Allen the lifeless body of Star lay spread out on her bed. She still looked as beautiful as ever, in her hand the pick that Allen had given her the day they met. Allen reaches over to her and kisses her forehead, "I love you Star, and I promise you that whoever did this to you will pay. I promise you." Allen squeezes his jaw shut holding back his deadly rage. His heart is completely broken at the sight of this poor girl, the girl he fell in love with so hard.

"BOOM" from above the sound of a large object crashing to the floor fills the room. He hears the strange noise again and then a scream, "Help!"

"I know that voice!"

Allen covers the body of his fallen angel with a blanket and picks up his needle. He turns to look at Star's covered body, gritting his teeth still trying to hold back the despair. He rushes out of the room heading for the floor above him ready to kill anyone or anything that happened to come across his determined path.

Allen gets about ten feet out the door when he is confronted by a tall skeletal figure. This creature stands close to seven feet tall. Allen tries to go around the monster but is blocked completely.

"Get out of my way!"

Allen lowers his head and makes a mad dash down the hall; he dodges and weaves his way around the creature finally locking himself behind the door in an adjoining room to avoid the danger. With one giant swing the beast smashes the door apart knocking it completely off of the frame sending Allen flying towards a window located in the back of the room. The needle in his hand and his only weapon is sent flying out the window and shatters loudly below. Allen shakes the cobwebs from his brain to see the giant thing entering the room, its sharp claws ready to impale him. Allen quickly searches the room for any kind of weapon but sees nothing of any protective value.

"What the hell!"

Allen suddenly pictures himself as a Matador and the creature as a bull. He stands to his feet ready to face this unholy creation head on.

"Come and get me you bastard!"

With that the monster sprints towards Allen arms outstretched. At the very last possible moment Allen dives completely out of the path of the monster. The creature attempts to slow its progression but finds itself flying through the window frame at about twenty miles an hour. As it descends through the window it reaches its spindly arm back into the room wrapping around Allen's ankle. In an instant the weight of the monster pulls Allen skyward toward the window. He reaches with all of his might grabbing onto the window sill trying to avoid being pulled to his death. Luckily for Allen the creature though very tall is not very heavy, that being said, his ankle was being torn into by the monsters long claws.

"Ahhh!"

Allen screams in agony. The pain filling his senses completely. He kicks and kicks trying to release the creatures grip. After what seems as an eternity of pain and suffering the creatures grip finally begins to slip down to Allen's shoe. He shakes the converse vigorously trying to loosen the monster until finally the shoe comes completely off causing the beast to let out an awful screech as it falls to its demise. Allen pulls his body back through the window just as a loud splash was heard at the base of the tower, the splatter of the monster sounded as if an entire swimming pool had been dumped over the side. Allen, face up on the ground, grasps his ankle trying to stop the bleeding by using his sock as a tourniquet but its not working. The tears flowed from his face causing the poor boy to gag until he turns to his side and lay in the fetal position. He felt he had no more left but without his help Alison and all the remaining survivors would surely be doomed. The sky began to grow dark just as Allen's hope began to fade away.

"Star, help me not to give up!"

The cold floor felt soothing on his throbbing body, it was his only comfort.

# Fifteen

"We call you beast of the eternal fire." The chants of the men gathered at the Black Mass begin as a whisper and increase until it becomes an almost deafening yell. Samantha and Tyler stand there surrounded by their occultist followers.

Samantha raises her arms towards the sky and speaks, "Master we have completed the sacrifice of innocence begun in 1962. Accept our second offering of all the children's souls that your minions have taken on this very day." Tyler and Samantha lift their hoods revealing their new snake-like visage. The two stand their like ancient Egyptian Gods commanding the respect and fear of all those in attendance.

Samantha raises her hands and calls out to the circled Brotherhood, "Bring forth my daughter, the final sacrifice" She waits impatiently and then turns to Tyler, "Where is she? Where is the girl?" Samantha searchers the followers gathered with suspicion.

Tyler responds, "You have the same blood running through your veins as she does." The female creature, that moments ago, was a human being stands their utterly perplexed by his statement. Tyler pulls forth the sacred knife. Samantha stares at Tyler.

"What are you doing?"

He smiles and then suddenly plunges the knife into her heart twisting and turning it viciously. She lets out a loud hissing noise deafening all in attendance.

"I am the power now and not you!" Samantha pulls herself from the blade and falls to the ground, black blood pouring onto the ground below.

"You have betrayed me." She begins to scream an unearthly howl, the warm sludge flowing out of the wound, her face changing from reptile back to old woman.

"You wouldn't be the first one I've betrayed."

Tyler places his boot on her throat and begins to crush the woman's voice box. "Let it be known that I have destroyed the High Priestess and have taken power of the gate. I alone will control the beast."

Tyler takes his foot from her throat and looks down at the fallen Priestess.

"The girl Alison will now be possessed by the beast instead of me. I will then be in control of her and the power within her."

Tyler walks around the inner circle of the Brotherhood fiercely portraying himself as the Alpha and the Omega. "Samantha will take the place as the blood sacrifice. Her blood will suffice as well."

Tyler now being the only one not completely frozen with fear reaches down to pick up the knife, he licks the black blade dry. The serpent man raises the knife high above his head; his followers fall to the ground and begin to give homage to him. "I have the key of eternity." One of his followers brings forth the sacred crystal skull and it is quickly filled with the blood of Samantha and taken out of the room. The sacred book is then revealed as well.

"Now get Alison and bring her to the cemetery, where I will drink her mother's blood and the door will open. We must hurry because the time of the full moon is approaching."

The servants quickly leave to retrieve the girl. Tyler had no idea however that Alison had escaped from the cell and was looking for him as well.

Allen finally reaches the room where he had heard the loud noise above him moments ago before he had been attacked by the tall skeletal man. He smashes his shoulder into the door knocking it wide open. Allen is shocked to see him still alive.

"Help me Allen!" Chained to the wall hangs Goob. He is covered from head to toe with deep cuts and bruises. The two are not alone however; a third man carrying a dagger and wearing a dark robe stands between them.

"YOU BASTARD!"

Allen rushes the goon spearing him in the chest with his shoulder, knocking the wind out of the man and sending him crashing through twin glass leading to the balcony outside. Allen follows the main onto the balcony where the two begin to wrestle for control of the knife. Allen kicks the man in the groin causing him to crumple in agony. The man rises to his feet elbowing Allen in the jaw bone causing a loud crack to resound inside his head. Allen's torso falls over the balcony railing releasing a stream of blood from his mouth. The assailant then grabs Allen's neck from behind trying to strangle him to death. Allen reaches down on the balcony floor trying to pick up the knife while retaining consciousness. Black spots appear in the center of his vision as he slowly loses his battle.

"Not like this."

With his last ounce of strength Allen pincers the knife with his index and middle finger up into his palm. He lunges backwards thrusting the blade into the man's stomach. The black spots slowly disappear as the man's grip weakens; Allen stands to his feet just in time to see his attacker take a nose dive over the railing.

The screams of the falling man last for a second until he hits the hard concrete seven stories below. Alison dives out of the way as the falling corpse lands mere inches from crushing her skull as she walked below. She looks to the sky to see where this flying man came from but sees nothing else above. Alison had to hurry now, time was of the essence.

Allen runs back into the room where his friend was hanging and grabs a hammer the evil man was no doubt going to use to torture and bludgeon his friend to death with. He begins to smash the chains that hold him confined to the wall. In a few moments Goob falls to the floor as he is finally released from the chains.

"Thanks for saving me. These guys dressed in black pulled me out of Xona's room and drug me here; it was right before we were going to make out!"

Goob was always thinking about girls, no matter what hell raising conditions surrounded him; his hormones were constantly in overdrive.

"Goob I need to find the men that killed Star."

Goob places his hand on Allen's shoulder, "Allen, I'm sorry about Star but are you crazy? Those guys will muderlize us!" Goob scans the room, "Let's look for a place to hide or just high tail it out of here." Goob gets on his knees in a pleading motion, "Dude, we can still escape with our lives! Please let's go now!"

Allen shakes his head, "No Goob, I'm gonna kill them all for what they did to her." Allen gives Goob a man hug, "Francis, leave if you want to but I have to stop those men, they are planning on opening a gate to Hell. I have to stop them and actually do something important for once in my life. If I don't then no one else will."

After nearly being flattened by the falling man Alison is forced to dive for the cover of a nearby bush as Tyler and his followers come bursting forth from within the main tower exit nearly spotting her but paying no attention to the splattered body of one of there so called brothers. Suddenly Tyler stops seemingly smelling something in the air with his long serpent tongue. He scans the area seemingly picking up the smell of Alison's blood and sweat mixture that now covers her body like sun tan lotion.

The evil leader turns his attention now back to face his men, "You have all served me well and have shown great strength and fortitude but your time has now sadly reached an end." The dark men look at each other with complete confusion, what did he mean come to an end?

Tyler raises his hand releasing a loud hissing noise. The men stand there dazed and confused, looking at each other for an explanation; from across the court yard a black galloping figure approaches them. The same beast that had chased Alison and Allen in the drain earlier was now unleashed on his own followers. Tyler and the hidden Alison watch as the helpless men are torn to pieces by the ravenous and extremely hungry beast. Tyler laughs with vigor as the beast consumes the flesh and bones of his own men.

"I will not share my glory with anyone." Tyler once again smells the air acting as if he were a bloodhound. He slowly walks towards the thick bushes hiding the extremely frightened Alison. He begins to run his hands through the underbrush feeling for the unseen woman, his long tongue pulsating back and forth into the cold air searching for any signs of life.

"I smell blood!"

"Ahh!!"

Alison screams in agony as she feels a giant sting on her right leg; she turns to see the underworld dog creature behind her on the other side of the bush. The creature again bites Alison this time purposely dragging her out from behind the bushes. Tyler reaches down to the poor woman and grabs her; throwing her over his shoulder like a sack of potatoes. He slowly carries her away; he had found his prize and was now ready to complete his devious and utterly evil plan to bring forth an opening between our world and Hell. He wanted power over all, and he knew he was closer than ever to making that a reality. Alison kicked and squirmed but to no avail, Tyler was now too powerful to stop. The doglike creature continued to nip at her heels and her legs dangled to and fro.

"Your mother could not stop me and neither will you."

Tyler grabs Alison by the neck turning her face upon his ghastly visage.

"You are the key to my immortality and yet your life is about to end. Thank you for sacrificing all that you have unto me. I guarantee that it will hurt! It is time now."

The snake man turns slowly and with complete confidence as he enters down the pathway leading to the old cemetery, the hound of hell follows him closely

licking his lips. Alison could not move a muscle it was as if she was paralyzed; she was transfixed by what used to be Tyler Hoffman but what was now some kind of snake creature, his familiar voice the only clue to the man behind the horrible mask. All is hopeless to her as she could not even lift a finger to fight him. The evil force was dominating. At last she had begun to accept her fate it was a fate that had been waiting for her all along. Alison may have prolonged the inevitable but the inevitable was inevitable. The full moon shone above her illuminating her dire predicament. The silhouette of flying bats filled the sky.
Sixteen

The two boys emerge from the main building carrying heavy torture hammers.
Goob searches the courtyard and finds that it is clear, "Let's get out of here Allen. Let's leave this place" Goob cannot stand the place any longer.
Allen also scans the courtyard with his eyes looking for any signs of danger, "Goob, I met a lady in the drain pipe; her name was Alison, she was trying to stop these bastards, we need to find her. She could still be alive."
Goob, knees shaking and all, responds "I just want to live to go to another rock concert." Seconds later the scream of a woman can be heard coming from the cemetery.
"What was that?"
Allen turns towards the cemetery, "That's her, we have to help her." Allen jumps down the stairs and makes his way towards the location of the scream.
"Hey wait up."
Goob takes a huge breath, filled with fear and anxiety, he follows his friend cautiously. The two friends edge closer towards the mysterious scream.
As Allen and Goob make their way around the bending trail they can hear the sounds of a woman screaming in pain but then instantly those sounds are mixed with those of a large dog growling. Immediately they stop dead in there tracks as the noises of the creature become to close to ignore. Allen spots a long stick on the side of the trail so he reaches down to pick up the wooden object, now carrying a weapon in both hands.
"OH MY GOD!"

The claws of the beast dig deep into the back of his shoulder sending the poor boy crashing to his face. Instinctively he rolls onto his back kicking at the creature which now has him mostly pinned to the dirt trail; letting out a Tarzan like scream Goob jumps the creature from behind punching and even biting at the thick hind fur. The monster turns its head extending its neck like a snake; grabbing Goob by his face and ripping his flesh apart. Goob's limp body falls off of the beast landing nearby. He has perished.

"GOOB!"

Allen's lungs are now burning with fire as he screams out in sadness. The creature grabs Allen by the blood soaked collar and drags him over to where Goob has fallen and places him atop his broken frame. The creature lets out a loud victorious howl. Allen is horrified when the jaws of the creature seem to unhinge and drop completely to the ground creating a mouth so cavernous that the beast could easily swallow the two whole. Slowly the beast begins to advance towards him, mouth wide open and ready for a feast of human flesh. The stench of his breath was that of rotting corpses.

The sound of a hand reaching into the puddle and then the crashing noise of a bull running through a glass wall emanates around the fallen victims. As the giant man-child swings a long blade cutting deep into the scalp of the dog creature the beast lets out a horrific painful yell and then falls onto the ground twitching and shaking. Bubba then grabs the hammer and twists it again while still lodged inside the beasts' brain.

"I hate dogs, especially ugly sons of bitches like this thing!"

The twitching stops and the creature lay completely silent. Allen is overjoyed at the sight of this large boy. He extends his hand and is lifted to his sore feet by his new best friend. He is shocked to see him still alive and even more shocked that Bubba had come to his rescue. Allen hugs his savior with great appreciation.

"Thanks Bubba, you saved my life."

Bubba responds, "Don't get all gay on me man! I don't know what came over me, I heard you guys screaming and I guess I had to do something. I have been hiding in those woods all day waiting for that thing to go away." Bubba reaches over and looks at the defeated monster, "Didn't he know that Bubba means Trubba!"

Allen falls to his knees trying to hold back his heartfelt tears.

"I'm gonna miss you Goob. I promise you didn't die in vain."

He grabs the other hammer from Goob's cold hand, "I'll miss you buddy, thanks." Allen continues towards the screaming Alison with Bubba right behind him.

As the two boys reach the cemetery they spot a figure standing over a grave both hands outstretched to the heavens holding an empty skull chalice.

"Now's my chance Bubba I need to nail him from behind."

Bubba grabs Allen by the shoulder, "Good Luck dick."

Allen responds, "If something happens to me get out of here."

Just as Allen rises to his feet the sound of thunder is heard cracking overhead. A large blanket of red clouds is crawling in from the four winds covering the entire sky. Droplets of rain fall onto the cemetery creating a river of mud around them. With the cloaked figures' back to him he rushes the tall man. What appears to be a red gate has begun to materialize out of one of the head stones in front of the standing Tyler Hoffman, it covers the entire cemetery ground with a red haze. Allen dives into the evil man and smashes his cloaked head or at least where his head should be, but there is nothing. The cloak falls to the ground empty and lifeless. Allen scrambles to his feet franticly looking around the cemetery for Tyler and Alison. He sees nothing but darkness.

"Where are you? Alison!"

He makes a gruesome discovery from behind one of the headstones; the decapitated body of Tyler Hoffman lay there in a shallow open grave. This was the original Tyler Hoffman and not his snake visage alter ego.

Allen wondered who could have done that to him, not that he didn't deserve it.

Allen yells out to Bubba but there is no response what Allen didn't know was that Bubba couldn't speak; his fat stomach has been disemboweled moments earlier.

The rain above has begun to intensify greatly. Allen looks down at his feet as a mound of dirt beneath him begins to move and shake it was like a tiny earthquake was surrounding him. Suddenly a slimy deformed arm shoots from the grave on which he is standing and begins to pull him into the ground. Allen scratches and kicks trying to escape but he is sucked in even further, he notices black roses scattered all around the head stone.

"Help, someone help me!"

Dirt begins to fill up around his neck, then his mouth and then the top of his head. Allen is quickly sucked completely beneath the dirt surface and into the grave. The air has become still without a sound in the night sky, the cemetery has transformed back into a lifeless arid desert. Black roses that now cover the new grave of young Allen sit as a reminder of the many tortured souls that have come and gone over the countless years since that fateful night in 1962 when Dr. Thomas Henderson went on his killing rampage trapping the souls of his innocent victims inside the cursed cage of the Asylum.

As if a child was being born out of the Earth Allen's finger tips and then his arms begin to emerge from the dark ground. He pulls his head out of the dirt and takes a babies' first breath. Allen gags and expands his lungs even further.

Allen releases a primal scream as he feels the tug on his leg once more pulling back down into Dr. Henderson's grave; the man's tortured soul would not allow him to release his victim.

Allen's fate appeared once more to be sealed but just when it seemed that all hope had been lost a brilliant blue light appears above Allen's outstretched fingers The mysterious light begins to create a blue whirlwind all around him sucking him from the grave and sending him flying half way across the graveyard but out of the reach of Thomas Henderson's grave. Allen is physically and emotionally shaken. He stumbles to his feet where the horrifying view of a possessed Alison comes into his field of vision. Allen realizes what has happened. Tyler had drunk the blood and now the Beast had entered into his friend and possessed her. It was also evident that the Beast had no use for an asshole like Tyler and so he ended him quickly. Allen had to help Alison resist the monster that was in full possession of her body now.

"Alison you have to fight him! Remember who you are, don't let him use you."

The mouth of Alison opens but it is not her sweet voice that echoes forth,

"You are too late boy I have entered your world and taken possession of a vessel."

Allen tries to run from the Beast but giant wings sprout forth from her back turning her into a dragon creature. The possessed woman quickly closes the gap between the two and in seconds has the boy in a vice grip. She lifts him from the ground and begins to squeeze his throat choking Allen to death slowly.

Allen is able to speak a few muffled words as he is being choked,

"Save us God, please save us."

The words seems to have a strange effect on the woman as a single tear falls from her dark eye at hearing his plea; the salty liquid slides down her cheek and as if it were in slow motion it sparkles all the way to the grave below. In the sky above the clouds begin to part and the night darkness turns back into day once more. A bright light emanating from the red clouds above strikes the winged-creature in the chest covering it in a blanket of white energy. Allen is dropped to the ground immediately; he coughs and sucks down air trying to regain his faculties. The light holds the creature in place covering its body as if washing it clean. The creature was completely immobilized by the heavenly power.

Allen notices that hundreds of unknown children or at least their spirits have surrounded the graveyard and are gathered there watching him and his struggle with the possessed woman demon. Allen squints his eyes and notices his beloved Star standing among the many souls. They stand there silent and pale as snow watching to see the outcome that would affect them for all of eternity. Alison has finally returned to her normal form except for her eyes, they remain black as night. The bright overpowering light from the clouds above disappears and the woman falls to her knees.

Behind the fallen woman Allen notices a small child with a blue glow carrying a knife, the child leans over and whispers into her ear. Alison nods her head in agreement with the mystery child and then looks towards Allen, her black eyes still chilling Allen to the bone. Allen instinctively knows what she is about to do. He rushes to stop her.

"It's the only way to set them free."

She slowly rises to her feet.

"He is trapped inside me for now but I can't hold him forever." Alison takes the knife from the small boy and drives it deep into her own chest.

"No!"

Allen screams as he reaches her fallen body. He cradles the dying Alison O'Connell in his arms.

"Why God? Why am I still alive when everyone else is dead?"

Alison gasps for breath and then answers him softly, "If I die then he will die with me and the souls of the children will be set free and the gate will close forever."

She begins to recite the ancient words from memory coughing up blood as she speaks them, "Dame es contas, eskenus lom antes." The red clouds that had formed above slowly dissipate as does the rain. A bright yellow sun begins to fill the sky even though it should be night. Allen holds Alison in his arms and watches as the souls of the children surrounding them slowly are taken up into the sky like shooting stars. The children disappear into the atmosphere like water vapors.

A loud growl begins beneath the Asylum buildings, the dirt and concrete rumbles like elephants stampeding and then as if the Earth were hungry the structures are slowly swallowed up by their very foundations, it was like witnessing Armageddon. The headstones surrounding Allen and Alison are also swallowed up by a tall green grass that acts more like a slithering snake. In a moment the cemetery is nothing more then an open grassy field. The past seems to fade into the hollow abyss of nothingness.

"It is finished, they are free."

Allen looks down to discover that Alison has passed on as well. He pulls her closer to him and shuts her eyelids for the last time.

"Thank you."

Just as quickly as it had begun, the lights, the rain, the thunder and the pain in her heart, it had ended. Alison could feel the sensation of a kiss on her cheek; she opens her eyes to see Jeremy standing there. Her brother stood there tall and handsome and without pain or scars on his face, she had never seen him like this. Jeremy reaches out his hand to Alison and beckons her to follow. Instantly she is lifted off of her feet and carried away from the cemetery and into what appears to be a blue hallway floating over the ground, as the two make there way into this mystical vortex Alison sees the blurry visage of an old man at the end of the tunnel she knew who it was, it was her father.

A voice can be heard inside her head, "It all comes back to you. A new door has been opened." She was finally home with her father and her brother, now she could rest in peace. Alison looks back one more time at her old life, she could see Allen sitting in the field holding her body as the wind blew the green grass around them; she smiled once more and then walked into the light.

# Sixteen

"BZZZZZZZZZZZZ," Alison leaps from the covers, sweat pouring down her face.

"Where am I?" The confused girl searches around her room. It was her bedroom, Mango barked and nibbled at her heels as her feet dangled over her bed. Alison can see and hear the TV that she had apparently left on; the reporter's voice fills the room.

"Today Doctor Thomas Henderson was a local hero, as the Valley Children's Hospital was being engulfed in flames the brave Doctor risked his life by pulling the sick children from there beds. All of the patients were saved from the flames by the heroism of Doctor Henderson and the Valley Fire Department."

Alison grabs the remote from her nightstand and changes the channel.

"Welcome to the Music Network. Well, they did it, the local valley band "Asylum" led by Singer Goob, guitarist Bubba Rhodes and Drummer Xona have just finished there first world tour. Lead singer Goob had this to say,"

"Rock and Roll is here to stay forever. Oh, did I mention I'm single ladies?"

Alison's jaw drops to her covers, "What is going on?" She hops to her feet and runs into the bathroom; looking into the mirror she could see her face, same features as ever. She rubbed her hands all around her face checking for anything out of the ordinary.

She pinched her arm, "Ouch, I'm awake, I'm me, I'm home."

"Knock, Knock."

It was a loud bang at her door. Alison grabs a robe covering her body and walks into the entrance hallway. Looking through the peephole she can see nothing.

"Hello, who's there?"

No response, just another knock on the door, this time even harder. Alison grabs the lock and turns it inward. A strong feeling of fear begins to fill her throat; she takes a big gulp then opens the door.

"Surprise!"

A man bursts through the door grabbing Alison from the floor lifting the startled woman from her feet and swinging her all around.

"Help!"

Alison screams out for assistance.

Quickly she is placed back on the floor, "Hey, it's me Pops."

Alison rubs her eyes then finally looks the man in the face; it was her father. He was old and wrinkled but it was her real daddy alright.

"Hey honey, we're here." Still in complete shock from seeing her much missed father, Alison looks towards the front door to witness her mother enter her home followed by a tall handsome young man.

"Hey dear guess who I brought? Your brother! He came down all the way from Maine to help us celebrate your birthday today!" Alison smiles and embraces her mother and then her beloved brother Jeremy, almost choking him with her affection.

"Glad you could make it Jeremy."

He smiles, "Me too, Thanks Alison." Alison pulls back from her embrace and gives him a strange look.

Jeremy smirks, "We're all thankful to you Alison."

As if a parade were taking place in her living room another knock is heard at the door, "Hey Ally baby." It was John; he looked like he always did; Hawaiian shirt and ponytail.

"Sorry I'm late Ally, Happy Birthday babe."

He places his hands on the shoulders of a young girl standing in front of him. "I brought my daughter Star with me. She wanted to know if Allen was going to be here."

"Allen?" Alison looks unsure of the name.

"Ally, your son, Allen." The little boy you popped out a few years ago." As if given the cue to show himself, a young boy comes running out of the back room.

"Mommy." He grabs Alison by the leg squeezing her tight and then releasing her grip. Star walks over to Allen, "Want to play?" Allen grabs Star by the hand and the two excited children run into Allen's playroom.

Alison begins to shed tears of joy not knowing what to think of any of this. She is able to create a bit of laughter inside her head, "So this is what was meant by a second chance at life." Alison hugs John,

"So you're not in any secret society or anything, are you John?"

John scratches his head, "I thought I was the crazy one around here. I was wrong." Alison gives John a serious look; causing his joyful giggle to cease.

"John, where is Tyler Hoffman?"

John looks around the room at the family members gathered, then settles his stare at her, "WHO?"

She smiles, "No one, I guess I just had a bad dream last night. I think that everything is going to be just fine." Alison's family and friends settle into the living room. She couldn't help but wonder two things; was she the only one who knew what had really happened in some distant past, in some weird dimension of what used to be there lives and the other important question, did she have a boyfriend now too? She laughed to herself as she closed the front door. She was ready to start her knew life with the father she had lost, a brother she had never known and the sweet blessing of her new child Allen. The sun shone over the city as the storm clouds that had been raging the night before seemed to roll out of sight exposing the beauty of the clear blue sky above.

Alison spends the entire day laughing and talking with her family. Life was now great again. That night she tucks her young son into bed and kisses him sweetly on the forehead.

"Goodnight Allen, I love you."

Alison turns off his night light and enters into her bedroom. She slips comfortably into her bed and passes into sleep; it was the best sleep ever. Mango curled up at her toes.

"CRASH!"

Alison is instantly awoken by the sound of glass breaking around her; she lifts her head to see a man invading her room. He is dressed in a white Doctor's jacket and is carrying a large weapon in his hand. Alison looks down at her arms and legs to discover that she is tied down to the hospital beds with straps; her body is that of a twelve year old child. She notices the man's name tag, Dr. Thomas Henderson. She searches the room with her eyes but it is no longer her bedroom it is a hospital room, or more appropriately it is an Asylum room. The calendar on the wall reads December 11th 1962. Alison screams in terror.

Thomas Henderson slowly approaches her bed with gun in hand.

"I'm sorry but I want my son back! They promised to bring him back!"

He roughly places the weapon into her mouth.

"Boom."

Alison hears a ringing sensation and then nothing. The reality was that she had been a patient at the Asylum all along, one of her multiple personalities was Alison O'Connell a famous reporter and yet another one was Alex Hoard evil avenger and others called Allen and Star. Alison had spent the last five years of her life living at the Asylum, creating these characters in her head. The only real thing was that there was a Dr. Henderson and he was really homicidal. Alison had been abandoned by her family and in a mental defense from her brain she had created an alternative world, one in which she could be anyone she wanted. The poor girl's heavy medication had worn off and she was now back to reality, patient number 12111962.

Sadly, she had become Dr. Henderson's final victim on that fateful day. She had become the final victim of the Asylum. Two months later the Asylum was closed forever, Alison's small body was placed in the cemetery behind the Asylum. Black Roses were placed on her tombstone by some unknown stranger. It is said that every year on December 11th you can see the spirit of the little girl playing in the woods, finally living free, free from the Asylum.

# The End?

Printed in the United States
115127LV00003B/287/P